HIS PLEDGE TO CHERISH

A SILVER STAR RANCH ROMANCE

SHANAE JOHNSON

THOSE JOHNSON GIRLS

CHAPTER ONE

A cool breeze swept a loose strand of hair across Saylor Silver's forehead. Her hair was normally pulled back from her head in a tight ponytail. The style was practical, allowing her a clear view to do her work with small and large animals.

She wasn't working in the barn this afternoon. There were no wounded animals about whinnying or squealing in pain. A joyous sound rang up as Saylor's older sister leaned forward to kiss her new husband.

Scout's grin was so big, her blue eyes so bright and filled with love, that Saylor felt the warmth even though it wasn't directed at her. Lincoln Rawlings, Saylor's new brother-in-law, smiled down at his bride as he met her lips. The crowd of family and friends cheered and whooped at the display of affection. When the couple broke the kiss, Linc looked at Scout in wonder, as though he still was in disbelief at his luck in finding the woman standing before him, accepting his vows to honor, protect, and cherish her until his last day.

More loose hair blew across Saylor's forehead. She swiped at it with her fingers, taking a moment to wipe the wetness from her eyes. When she did so, she saw the man standing behind Linc do the same.

Jefferson Moore was Linc's best man. Like most soldiers, his hair was cut close to his scalp. Meaning no strands of wayward hair blew into his face. Meaning there was no way he could brush the emotional movement off as moving his hair from his eyes. Unlike Saylor, Jeff didn't try to use his hair as a ruse.

With the index finger of his right hand, Jeff caught the moisture at his eyes. Then he caught her gaze. Saylor knew she should look away. Men didn't like women seeing them in times of weakness. Instead of frowning at the intrusion, Jeff offered her a grin.

It wasn't even a sheepish grin. It was a

conspiratorial grin. As though he saw her tears as well and was standing beside her in solidarity.

Saylor liked that feeling, the feeling of standing united with someone. Too often, she felt alone in this world. Though she was always surrounded. By her sisters. By the animals she tended to as a veterinarian.

And by the man in her life. Her boyfriend, Nick. Who was seated not too far away. But when she looked for him in the small crowd of seated guests on the bride's side, she saw no hide nor hair of him.

Had he left? He'd told her he hated weddings. He'd told her that they were boring and self-indulgent and a waste of time. She'd begged him to come. It had taken days for him to relent and agree. And now he was gone.

No, wait. She caught sight of his red hair. He'd moved to the groom's side of the aisle. Perhaps he was making nice with Linc's soldier buddies over there.

But no. Nick wasn't rubbing elbows with straight-backed, broad-shouldered men with buzz cuts. A woman flipped her dark hair over her shoulder as she leaned into him. Another touched his forearm to bring his attention back around to her.

When Nick lifted his head, his gaze didn't connect with hers. When he lifted his hand to brush the strands of red hair out of his face, his eyes gleamed. Not with tears. Any moisture would evaporate in the heated gaze he split between the two women.

Saylor jerked her gaze from the scene. When she turned her head, her eyes landed on Jeff. His mouth was pressed in a firm line of displeasure. Saylor's immediate thought was to wonder what she'd done wrong to him? Following Jeff's eye line, she saw what upset him.

Saylor wanted to assure Jeff that Nick wasn't being unfaithful. He was just a flirt. All men flirted. All men looked at other women. It didn't mean anything.

Look at her own father. Abe Silver had had three wives in ten years. That was normal, at least in her world.

Nick was an attractive man. Women were bound to notice. She couldn't expect him not to look. But Nick's attention always turned back to her. Just like her father had always come back to her mother. That was the true test of love, that they came back.

The sound of the Wedding March brought Saylor's attention back to the happy event. It was time for Linc and Scout to begin their walk down the aisle as newlyweds. Saylor's oldest sister, who had been her first friend, was now walking away with the new most important person in her life. Saylor stood on the raised platform, feeling utterly alone.

To the side of her, Saylor felt Father Matthews's gaze on her. He'd just officiated one marriage. Saylor was hoping he might preside over hers and Nick's. If the pastor saw Nick getting cozy with those two women, he might get the wrong idea.

But Father Matthews wasn't looking at her. He wasn't looking at Nick. He was grinning at Jeff and clapping him on the shoulder.

"I suppose you'll be next?" said Father Matthews.

"If only I'm so lucky," was Jeff's answer.

With his right hand, Jeff rubbed at his left arm. The left one was cradled in a sling, injured and numb after his last mission in the military, the one that had taken her father's life and brought The President's Men here to the Silver Star Ranch.

Those six men from her father's unit had only been here on the Silver Star Ranch for just over a week. And in that time, one of their own had met, fell in love with, and married the eldest daughter of their former commander.

It was General Abe Silver that had made his men promise to check on his six daughters just before he died. It was the General that had written in his will that in order for his daughters to keep the ranch, they each had to get married or the land and house they all had grown up in would go to their ex-step-mother who wouldn't hesitate to sell the land and pocket the profit. Catherine, or Cruella as the Silver sisters had taken to calling their step-mother, was still angry that her ex-husband had chosen to come back to his first wife.

That move hadn't surprised Saylor at all. First love never dies, her mother had told her. Nick was Saylor's first love. She would always come back to him.

Though he didn't rise to come to her now that the wedding was over.

Jeff held out his arm for Saylor. It was his right arm. Saylor hesitated but took his arm. As they began the walk down the aisle and toward the tables set out for the wedding reception, she didn't feel so alone anymore.

What she felt was tired. She wanted to close her eyes and follow Jeff's lead. She wanted to sink into the warm heat of him and fall asleep. She wanted to press her fingers into his hands and ask him to not let her go.

Saylor's eyes flashed open. She gave her head a shake to clear her mind. Where had those thoughts come from?

"You okay?" Jeff asked, his voice pitched low so that only she would hear.

"Of course," Saylor said. "Why wouldn't I be?"

"It's a big change. Your sister got married." Jeff gazed into her eyes, seeing more than she wanted him to. His smile was gentle. His features held no judgment of what she knew he'd seen. "Do you think you'll be next in line?"

Saylor wanted to laugh as much as she wanted to whimper. She wanted to be next in line. She'd wanted to be the first Silver sister to marry, ever since she was old enough to know what marriage meant.

She wanted a boy to look at her and choose her to be his wife, to be his love for the rest of their lives. "Yes, I do want to be next."

"Next for what?"

And just like that. The weariness she'd felt, the loneliness covering her shoulders, left her with the sound of his voice.

"Hey, Nick," Saylor said.

She let go of Jeff's arm and reached for her boyfriend's. Nick's hands were on his phone. His gaze as well. But he was here. He'd left those other women behind and come for her. He always came back to her.

"Next in line for marriage," said Jeff.

That brought Nick's gaze up. Saylor stood perfectly still in the silence. Another strand of her hair blew in front of her face, but her view was clear.

Instead of smiling at Saylor gently, Nick's brows shot up to his hairline. His lips turned down in a frown. His nose wrinkled as though he smelled something foul.

And then he burst out in laughter. "We're too young to get married. Personally, I don't plan to do that until I'm thirty-five at least. Gotta sow those oats, am I right?"

Nick lifted his hand for a fist bump.

Jeff did not raise his fist.

Nick looked down at Jeff's left hand, held securely in the sling. "Aw, sorry, man."

Nick didn't sound in the least bit sorry. Saylor's face burned at her boyfriend's manners. She wanted to explain to Jeff that Nick didn't always notice things. That he sometimes put his foot in his mouth.

That he wasn't always mindful of other people's feelings.

She didn't have the opportunity.

Jeff turned his back on Nick. His gaze focused on her. He lifted his right hand to her shoulder and gave her a squeeze.

"Save me a dance?" Jeff said.

Again, warmth spread through her at his touch. It was a calming, soothing warmth, much like a heated blanket on a cold night. Saylor couldn't remember the last time she'd slept through the night. She bet she could if Jeff were her blanket.

Again, she had to blink and shake off that errant thought. The shake of her head looked like she was declining.

"Oh, no," she rushed to say. "I mean, you don't have to."

Jeff offered her a tight smile. With a slight bow like something out of a historical novel, he straightened and turned on his heel. Taking with him the warmth and comfort and leaving her standing alone with Nick.

CHAPTER TWO

*J*eff massaged the flesh of his left arm. His right hand squeezed and kneaded, but he felt nothing. He wished the rest of him was so lucky. He had feelings all over his body. Mostly in his heart.

Since the first day here, since the first time he'd seen her, it seemed his heart was auditioning for the role of acrobat in a circus. It had flipped the first time Saylor Silver's gaze had landed on him. It had swung high when she'd smiled so sweetly at him as she was introduced to the men in his unit. The smile was small as it had to stretch to greet all six of the President's Men. There hadn't been any interest in him in the curve of her lips. Just politeness.

Saylor was polite. She was kind. She was thoughtful.

When her gaze slipped to his limp arm, her brows had drawn. Not in morbid fascination like some. Or idol curiosity like others. Nor even wanton pity like a few women he'd meant in the past months. Lonely women who looked at him with a calculating gaze that they could nurse him and earn his undying love.

Jeff had no interest in such an exchange. For him, love was unconditional. Not transactional. There was no tit for tat. Only an open heart given freely with a no returns policy.

So when his gaze met Saylor Silver's and his heart dropped into his gut, he knew.

Saylor had looked at him and smiled. She'd looked at his arm and calculated. But those calculations weren't on how to indebt Jeff to her. Saylor saw an injury she wanted to heal because it was simply her nature.

Over the past week, he'd seen how she stayed up forty-eight hours straight with an elderly, pregnant mare. Soothing the old girl as she'd birthed her last foal. He'd watched from a distance as she'd splinted a chicken's broken foot. The other guys had been disappointed they wouldn't be having chicken salad for lunch.

Unfortunately, Saylor's healer's soul extended to the undeserving kind of animal as well.

Jeff spied The Boyfriend across the outside dance floor. The Boyfriend, that's what Saylor's sisters called him. Not one of the Silver sisters even deigned to use the man's name.

The Boyfriend's hand slid down a woman's forearm. It came to rest at her lower back. And then dipped farther.

None of that would be a problem. If the bottom in question where The Boyfriend's hand now rested belonged to his girlfriend.

It wasn't Saylor's bottom. Saylor was sitting down in a chair, not too far away from the display. She had a clear sight of what was going on. Instead of getting up and marching over to her boyfriend, she turned her back to the scene. Taking a deep breath, she plastered on a bright smile.

Even from across the space, Jeff could tell that the smile didn't reach her eyes. It was dull and heavy. It was fogged and unfocused, trying to erase what she'd just seen.

Jeff knew the look all too well. His mother had

worn that look whenever they were out in public. Women in their small town had snickered behind their hands or looked at her pityingly.

Audrey Moore had worn a serene smile as though she were oblivious to her husband's indiscretions. But Jeff had seen what his father was up to. He'd also seen the bruises his mother tried to hide along with her heartbreak.

Saylor had no bruises that Jeff had seen. All of her hurts appeared to be internal. He knew for a fact that those hurt the worst.

He clenched his right fist, wishing he could shove it down The Boyfriend's throat. But then that would make him no better than his father. Even worse, he had a sinking suspicion that it wouldn't change Saylor's view of her cheating ex.

So instead of punching The Boyfriend, Jeff massaged his left forearm. The nerves there were frayed and not getting the signals. Just as his heart wasn't getting the signal that any pursuit of Saylor Silver was a fruitless endeavor.

"There you are."

Jeff looked up to see the bride walking toward him. The sun had set on Scout and Linc's wedding day, but the party was only just getting started.

"I was hoping you would dance with my sister," said Scout.

Jeff perked up at that. He'd asked Saylor to save him a dance. But he hadn't managed to make his way to her yet. He'd been far too busy watching the antics of her boyfriend, much like Saylor pretended she wasn't doing.

"You should dance with Brig." Scout shoved her youngest sister into Jeff's arms.

With his attention still on Saylor, Jeff nearly didn't catch Brig. Luckily, the young woman wore cowboy boots and not heels, so she was able to steady herself in his one-handed catch.

Brig turned to glare at her oldest sister. Scout winked at the youngest Silver before wrapping her arms around her husband and tugging him a short distance away. Linc shrugged apologetically at Jeff before following his wife's lead.

"Looks like you drew the short stick," said Brig.

"Pardon?" said Jeff.

"Scout wants you with me because she thinks you're the most harmless."

Jeff knew that Scout was trying to set up all of her single sisters in an effort to meet her father's deadline. If all six of the Silver sisters weren't married in three months, then the ranch would go to their stepmother, whom Jeff understood wanted to sell the ranch for a profit and kick them all off.

"Harmless?" Jeff parroted. "Me?"

"Yup."

Scout had no idea how wrong she was. Jeff had had a reputation of loving them and leaving them up until a year ago. All of the President's Men had a similar reputation before their separation from the military. They each had kept their lives small and contained enough to fit in a duffle bag. A woman couldn't fit in that baggage.

"I don't believe it, though," said Brig. "You're too quiet to be harmless. My dad said always watch out for the quiet ones."

"You're not quiet either," Jeff said as he gave Brig a twirl.

Brig's face split into a grin, confirming his suspicion. "I'm also not the Silver sister you've got your eye on, am I?"

Jeff couldn't help it. He lifted his gaze. He found her immediately. He always knew exactly where Saylor was. She was like a beacon for him.

She was standing now. Talking with an older lady. But Saylor's gaze kept dipping back to The Boyfriend.

The cheater was still in conversation with the

brown-skinned woman. At least his hands weren't on her body. They were on his phone as he tapped at the keys. The woman tapped at her phone as well. Were they exchanging numbers?

"I think we could help each other," said Brig. "In fact, I think you can help us all."

"Help?" said Jeff, his mind not processing Brig's words as he watched Saylor's carefully blank features crumble. "How?"

"We need to get rid of him."

Jeff didn't need to ask who Brig meant by *him*. He also knew it was likely a fool's errand. Saylor clearly knew what was happening beneath her nose. Those in abusive relationships often did. Because make no mistake, cheating on one's partner was emotional abuse.

A woman's reasons for staying with a man who hit her or called her names wasn't often very different from staying with a man who betrayed her trust. Trying to separate an abuse victim from an abuser was a tricky mission. One Jeff had failed at before.

"We can't get rid of him," said Jeff, though it was a bitter pill to swallow. "She has to make that choice."

"Does she look like she's happy?"

The Boyfriend wasn't looking down at his phone any longer. He was on the dance floor. He pressed his body against the woman who was not his girlfriend as she shimmied in front of him.

The smile on Saylor's face slipped. She was clearly holding tears back. This time they weren't the joyful kind as when she'd watched her sister kiss her new husband. Jeff had let his own tears fall at that happy occasion.

No, Saylor did not look happy now.

"Why is she even with him?" asked Jeff.

"He was her first boyfriend. She keeps going back to him. Just like mom did with our dad. In case you haven't noticed, we all have daddy issues."

Jeff couldn't understand why? He would've killed to be raised by a man like the General. Instead, he was raised by a monster who liked to put his hands on his mother.

Jeff felt a tingle in the palm of his left hand. From time to time, the numbness receded, leaving him with a shock of sensation. He no longer had hope that he would get the full use of his arm back. But if he could use it just once more, he knew exactly what he'd do with it.

No, he wouldn't use it to commit violence. He would use it to sweep Saylor Silver off her feet and carry her away from that poor excuse of a man. Then he'd wrap her up tight and never let her go.

But that was just a dream. She stood immobile, unreachable on the other side of the dance floor. He stood numb, watching her.

CHAPTER THREE

*S*aylor's face was tired. Her vision blurred with the strain of staying open. Her lips split with a dry crackling sound under the pressure of the fake smile she'd been holding on to all throughout her sister's wedding reception. Her forehead ached from the pressure of projecting the pretense that she was perfectly happy and content with her lot in life.

She wasn't. But it was fine. She would manage.

Saylor sat off to the side of her mother's garden, alone and unnoticed. Meanwhile, Linc spun Scout around and around in dizzying circles that made her older, no-nonsense sister giggle. Saylor couldn't remember the last time she'd heard Scout giggle. She couldn't remember the last time her own lips stretched so far in a smile of complete happiness. But she supposed the love of a good man would do that to a girl.

Saylor's gaze skated to the other side of the make-shift dance floor. It looked like her own man was having a good time now. Saylor watched him move and shake his body in time to the beat.

Nick was a great dancer. He had a natural rhythm and grace. The first and only time Saylor had tried to match his moves, he'd laughed at her.

Which had been fine since he hadn't been the only one. Everyone around them at the high school dance had laughed at her. Saylor had feigned a twisted ankle and sat the rest of the song out. She never got up to grace a dance floor again.

Which was why her boyfriend was dancing with his ex Holly Marks and his other ex Kellie Dustin. The two women moved their hips and shimmied their shoulders on either side of him. Nick spun first Holly, who he'd dated in junior year, and then Kellie, who Saylor was certain she'd seen him out with in their junior year as well.

They were all still friends even after the drama of high school. They still hung out from time to time. Even a couple of overnight trips to beaches and ski resorts.

Saylor bet they were fun. She wouldn't know.
She hadn't been invited. Nick thought she'd feel
awkward around the group she'd never been part of.
Which had been fine because Saylor always had
tons of work to do at the ranch and tending to the
injuries of other animals in the county as a
veterinarian.

Nick pulled Holly close and dipped her in a
move Saylor had always wanted to try. But with her
two left feet, she was sure she'd take both herself
and her partner crashing down to the dance floor.
Nick and Holly managed the steps, their bodies
pressed so tight together that she couldn't get a dime
between them.

Which was fine. Just fine.

It was good for him to get out and socialize now
that he was unemployed. It wouldn't do either of
them any good if he were up under her every day
seeking attention. It was good for him to seek
attention elsewhere. When people clung in
relationships, it tended to suffocate them.

Saylor let out the breath she was holding as Nick
held Holly close as the two of them slowly swayed to
the beat of the fast-paced song. Nick whispered
something in Holly's ear, and she grinned. The
music was too loud, which explained why they were

dancing so close. So that they could hear each other.

Which was fine.

Because any minute now, Nick would come back to her. Likely after this song played. Then a dance hit from when they were all in school came on. Everyone threw up their hands and started a choreographed series of movements.

Saylor stayed in her seat, tapping her foot in time to the rhythm. She licked at her bottom lip, trying to keep it from cracking under the pressure of her smile. And then, just as she'd predicted, Nick made his way over to her at the end of the song.

"You look tired, babe." Nick reached his hand out to her cheek.

Saylor rested her cheek in his palm. His hand was sweaty and smelled of two different brands of perfume that clashed with each other and turned her stomach. But she didn't turn her head away from the man she loved.

"Those bags under your eyes are not cute," said Nick, tilting his head to the side and regarding her. "You should call it a night."

"Sure," said Saylor as she rose. "Just let me say good night to my sisters. I'll meet you at the car, and we can head to your place."

"Oh, no-no." Nick held up his hands. "No need for you to drive back into the city. Why not stay here with your family tonight?"

"Because I'm sure my sister, the newlywed, wants some privacy with her new husband."

Nick scratched at his chin. "Well, it's just that I'm not ready to call it a night yet. And I don't want to drag you out."

"I'll come out with you. I'll just grab a cup of coffee. Besides, there's something I wanted to talk with you about."

Nick bit at the inside of his lip. His gaze was over Saylor's shoulder. When she turned, she saw Holly and Kellie waiting against the back gate. Their grins were tilted up, their eyes cast down in that way of the two gossiping girls Saylor remembered from high school.

"It was a nice ceremony, wasn't it?" said Saylor.

"Hmm?" Nick brought his gaze back to her. "Oh, yeah."

"It made me think about what I might want for my own ceremony."

Nick frowned down at her as though she were speaking in an alien tongue. "Your ceremony?"

Saylor swallowed. There was a fluttery feeling in her stomach. She and Nick had been dating for three years. Well, they had gone on their first date three years ago. Then he'd called her up three months after that. Then two months after that. It had taken a little over a year, but soon they were going out on a regular basis of a handful of times each month.

It wasn't the regularity that had sealed the deal. In Saylor's purse, she held what no other woman in his life had; a key to his apartment. He'd given it to her last winter when he'd come down with a nasty case of the flu. Saylor had dropped everything and nursed the man she loved back to health. When he was all better, he hadn't asked for the key back.

That had to be a sign.

She'd wanted to give it a few more months, maybe another year. But she no longer had the luxury of time. If she wanted to keep the ranch, and her job, and the horses she'd cared for since she was a girl, and her sisters with a roof over their heads, she had to get her boyfriend to marry her.

"Nick, you remember what I told you about my dad's will?"

He frowned again. His brows drawing in that cute V of confusion he'd always get when she'd tried to tutor him in math back in high school. That look that said he did not remember what she'd said to him just a minute ago.

"We all need to get married to save the ranch."

The V in his brow sprung upward into a flat line. Nick stepped back. "Look, Saylor, you know how I feel about you... But marriage? At my age?"

Well, at least he remembered their conversation. That was a good start. She just wished they were having this conversation out of earshot of two of his exes.

"Look, babe, you know I'm going to marry you."

The world stopped. Time stopped. Saylor's heart stopped.

It wasn't exactly a proposal because he didn't form it in a question. But that was fine. In fact, it was even better. To Nick, their marriage was a foregone conclusion, so he didn't need to ask.

"You know," he continued, "...someday."

"Well, the thing is, we all have to be married by the end of the year."

This time his brows scrunched together, in the way they did when he was trying to calculate a simple math problem.

"That's only three months away," Saylor supplied the answer for him.

Nick scrunched his lips together in the way he

did when he got the answer wrong. "I tell you what; if it's really that important to you, and all of your sisters get married in time, then we'll be the last ones to go. How's that?"

Again, it wasn't the most romantic of overtures, but Nick wasn't a romance kind of guy. He'd had difficulty spelling that word all the way back in elementary school. Roman, he could spell as it referred to soldiers. But he always added an S instead of the C and E.

Still, this was exactly what Saylor wanted. The guy she'd had a crush on since kindergarten, the guy she'd pined after all through middle school, the man she'd dreamed of all through high school was finally agreeing to spend the rest of his life with her.

It was too much. It was everything. Saylor couldn't form words. And so she nodded.

Nick pressed a soft kiss to her mouth. His lips tasted of cherry lip bomb, the kind Kellie was wearing. The sweet flavor was bitter on Saylor's tongue. She swallowed it down regardless.

"Why don't you go get some rest," Nick said after he pulled away from her. "You look dead on your feet."

Saylor looked over at Kellie and Holly, who were

moving toward the cars parked out back. "Where are you guys headed?"

Nick shrugged. "Just to catch up. Reminisce about old times. Stuff you weren't there for, so you'd be bored to tears."

Because Saylor hadn't run with the popular crowd back in high school. Or in college. Or, as it would have it, now.

"I'll call you, okay."

"Yeah, okay."

Nick turned and headed to his car with Holly and Kellie each taking one of his arms. They were already laughing and giggling as they left her behind.

Which was fine. Because Saylor actually was tired. She rubbed at her lower eyelids. She couldn't feel any bags there, but she did sense a wellspring of tears ready to spill over with any more pressure.

Saylor turned from the reception area. She didn't want to go into the house to the bedroom there. She wanted a few moments alone to gather herself. So, she headed to her cabin at the back of the house.

She should be happy. Nick was going to marry her. Her dreams were coming true. Everything was well and truly fine.

The sounds of her sister's wedding reception died down as Saylor reached the cabin's door. The sky was clear overhead, but Saylor felt drops running down her cheeks. She had to hurry inside before the deluge started.

She turned the knob and walked inside just in time. Tears poured from her eyes. Her sobs sounded like thunder in her ears. Luckily, she walked into a darkened area. But something moved in the darkness.

"Saylor?"

Lights came on, and she saw Jeff. He stood in the middle of the room. His jacket was off. His shirt open. His gaze wide and trained on her.

Saylor had thought her sobs sounded thunderous. They were nothing to the growl that escaped Jeff's clenched jaw. And then she was against his chest. A strong arm and two warm lips pressed to her forehead.

All of a sudden, Saylor didn't want to be anywhere but right where she was.

CHAPTER FOUR

*J*eff pulled Saylor tightly into his chest. His right forearm fit snuggly around her slight shoulders. His hand skated up to squeeze her shoulder cap. He felt a tingle in his left palm. The same tingle he'd felt the first time he'd seen her. The same tingle he'd felt when she'd tended to his slight wound last week. The same tingle that arose each time he saw her face, heard her voice, or simply thought about her.

Because, yes, just the mere thought of Saylor Silver could bring feeling to every part of him. Including the part that had been ravaged by an explosion. Jeff closed his eyes as he held this burst of sunlight to him. Behind his eyelids, he would've sworn he saw stars.

She sniffled against his chest. Her hands were balled into fists that lay at his sides. But she didn't appear to be pushing him away. That was a good sign because he wasn't sure he could've let her go. Instead of moving away from him, Saylor turned her head and buried herself more deeply into his chest.

Her breaths against his bare skin should've heated him through. Her soft cheek on his beating heart should've made his desire spike. Instead, all Jeff could feel was white, hot anger coursing through his veins.

He was going to kill Nick.

Yes, Nick and not The Boyfriend. Jeff was using the man's name. Most of the casualties of war were nameless bodies left behind as the spoils of battle. But not this one. For this traitorous villain, Jeff would look directly into his eyes just before he wrung his neck.

The desire to do violence caused the pinky of his left hand to twitch. Not even his feelings for Saylor had brought that much feeling in him. But the thought of doing harm to Nick did. With that thought, Jeff's ire instantly cooled.

For most of his life, he'd been an angry kid. Needing to put his fists against anything and anyone who moved against him. Because he could not protect himself or his mother at home.

It wasn't until he'd joined the Armed Forces that he'd learned to put that anger, that pain to use. General Abe Silver trained him as a soldier, ready and willing to take orders to combat the enemy the commander pointed at. Jeff learned to never raise his hand in anger, but only in a calculated plan sanctioned by his betters.

He was under no orders to attack The Boyfriend. The General had sent him here for one purpose. To make sure his daughters wanted for nothing. Saylor's tears told him that she ached for something she did not have. Jeff pledged he would do all he could to fill that need.

The anguish in Saylor's sobs gutted Jeff. He wanted to be able to wrap both arms around her and hold her securely. His left arm hung limp at his side, numb from the blast that had taken her father from both their lives.

Slowly by bits, Saylor's sobs tapered off until only her even breathing remained. As she quieted, she didn't let Jeff go. At some point, her fingers had unballed from fists. They now wrapped around his back. Her hands clasped in a deadlock at the base of his spine.

Jeff knew he should say something comforting. But for the life of him, he didn't know what those words might be. He wasn't the best with words. A map and coordinates, certainly. But with the lines and curves that made up words instead of topography, he was left directionless. And so he asked the stupidest question on the face of the earth.

"Are you all right?"

Of course, she wasn't all right. Jeff had seen that loser neglecting her all night. He'd watched as The Boyfriend had danced with not one but two other women, getting inappropriately close for someone in a committed relationship. All the while, Saylor had sat off to the side looking so lost.

Jeff had wanted to go to her, but he didn't have that right. And he knew any of the words he had for her would not be appreciated. Words like; *you need to leave him*, or *you deserve better than this.*

She did deserve better. But he knew that she wouldn't believe it. His mother never believed it. But Jeff wasn't sure if he could ever muster the strength to walk away from another victim of abuse.

At the sound of his voice, Saylor seemed to snap out of her fugue state.

"It's fine," she said. "I'm fine."

She unlocked her hands from his back. Her arms came from around him and snapped back to her sides.

"I'm sorry," she said, wiping at her eyes. "You must think I'm a complete basket case."

Jeff wanted to tell her he thought she was perfect. He wanted to bring her back into his arms. He wanted to kiss the dark bags under her eyes and hold her as she slept, taking all of her old baggage away from her.

"It's just the wedding was so beautiful... That's why I was crying. I got emotional."

Jeff nodded his head at her obvious lie.

"I wanted to give Scout and Linc their privacy, so I came to my cabin. I forgot you were staying here."

"It's fine," said Jeff. "You can stay here. I'll go next door to Scout's cabin."

He took a step and then froze. Saylor looked so lost standing in the middle of the room. Jeff wanted to reach for her, to pull her back to him. But he had no valid reason to. She was trying desperately to hide her pain.

He wanted her to know that she could never hide it from him. He knew that pain all too well. But because he knew the taste and texture of it, he knew that it did not want to be seen. And so he turned away, but not in the direction of the door.

"I was going to make a cup of hot tea with milk first. Do you mind? I could make you a cup as well."

In his peripheral vision, Jeff saw Saylor's shoulders relax. Just a bit. She didn't quite look up at him. But she nodded. And so Jeff put the kettle on.

CHAPTER FIVE

*S*aylor scrubbed at her face. The woman staring back at her in the bathroom mirror was unrecognizable. No, that wasn't true. She recognized herself all too well.

The make-up she'd carefully painted on her face to hide the blemishes had sweated off. Her hair, which normally was pulled back to show off the angles in her face, hung limp, making her face look fat and chubby. The bags under her eyes were so dark she looked like she'd been slapped in the face.

This was her. Saylor Silver. Second sister of the Silver girls. Second best beside her near-twin Mareen. It all added up to never being first. Not just in her family, but also in her lovelife.

Her own boyfriend, her first love, rarely put her

first. Which was fine. She wasn't begrudging Nick his friendships. She just wished he'd hang out with guy friends instead of two of his ex-girlfriends. Women who had been his loves before he'd even noticed Saylor.

"Saylor, do you want honey or sugar?"

And there was that. Saylor couldn't' believe she'd just cried in front of Jeff. Now, like the rest of the town who'd watched her boyfriend dance attention on two of his exes, Jeff knew how pathetic she was.

"Um, you decide," Saylor called out to him.

Because she knew better than to tell a man her desires. She'd already tried to get her boyfriend to consider marriage to her. At least Nick hadn't shot her down like she'd feared he would. He'd considered it. He'd even made it a possibility. Which meant she had no reason to be crying in another man's bathroom.

Saylor gave herself another glance in the mirror. There wasn't much she could do about her appearance. It wasn't like she was trying to impress Jeff. She had a boyfriend who would consider asking her to marry him in a few months.

Maybe.

If all her sisters got married first.

Which even she had to admit to herself was a long shot.

Mareen was engaged, so that was a done deal.

Brig was chomping at the bit to pick one of the soldiers.

Tilly was on board but going about it in a way that made Saylor cringe. If her younger sister wasn't careful, she would end up with a Russian mobster as a husband.

Not to mention Gunnery, who wasn't even on this continent and had no plans to return any time soon.

There was no way they could pull this off in three months. Meaning they were going to lose the ranch. And Saylor was likely to lose her chance at a husband.

"Tea's ready," called Jeff.

Saylor wiped at her face one last time. She left her hair dangling around her shoulders since she had no hair tie. It was the best she could do. Not that Jeff was in any way interested in her. He was just a kind man who was eager to help.

And so, Saylor trudged into the main room of the cabin she had built with her father, Scout, and Mareen. Mareen had hated every second of the exercise. She'd complained with each smudge of dirt she'd gotten on her clothing. Saylor hadn't been thrilled at the building project either. She'd much rather tend to the animals. But like good soldiers, the girls had done as the General commanded. The cabins had gone up and then been left empty at the back of the main house. Until these six soldiers came to stay.

Saylor found Jeff holding two mugs in one hand. He was on his way to the table Mareen had built. The piece of furniture was surprisingly sturdy for being built by a young girl who hated wielding a hammer.

"Let me help you with that." Saylor reached for the mugs, but Jeff had already set them down. Instead of meeting cool ceramic, Saylor's fingers brushed the warm mound of Jeff's bicep.

"I've got it," he said, giving her a smile.

The smile was simply a lift of one side of his mouth accompanied by a flash of straight white teeth. It should have brought to mind a predator. Perhaps a wolf, toying with its prey before sinking its teeth in.

Not for one moment did Saylor feel that Jeff was a threat. She felt safe. She felt protected. Which was odd since there was no danger in her life.

For his part, Jeff watched her. A wary expression

in his gaze. He glanced downward. Saylor was embarrassed to see that her hand still rested on his bicep. She was mortified to see that it lay on his left arm, the one he often carried in a sling.

"I'm so sorry," Saylor yanked her hand away. "That was so rude."

Her fingers felt branded, as though she'd just yanked them away from fire. Jeff's arm had been warm under her touch. She had expected the limb to be cold to the touch since he'd lost feeling in it. However, it had felt alive and vibrant.

"I would have considered it rude," he said. "If you were getting fresh with me."

Saylor looked up, mortified until she saw Jeff's grin. He was playing with her. Joking as she did with her sisters. Nick was never playful or jokey with her.

Jeff scooted back into the couch. His hand on the back would've brushed her shoulder if she leaned over. She had the urge to curl up next to him and enjoy the warmth of the sweet tea.

"Cold?" Jeff reached for a blanket.

Before Saylor could say anything, he'd flung it over her legs. She felt overheated, but not by the blanket. She wasn't used to having a man anticipate her needs, much less take care of them.

She spent her days looking after Nick, trying to

anticipate his needs. She also spent much of her free time cleaning his apartment. Nick was often careless about his things. Looking around the cabin, it looked spotless and tidy. There wasn't a thing for her to straighten up.

"I feel like I just lost you," said Jeff.

Saylor blinked until Jeff came into focus. His light brown eyes were focused on her face. That was another thing she wasn't used to. Nick often had his face buried in his phone, on the television, or looking at his surroundings when they were out. Saylor often caught him looking at the backside of a pretty woman as she walked by.

"Wanna tell me where you just went?"

"It's Nick." His name popped out of her mouth, unbidden.

"The Boyfriend."

"You say that like my sisters. They don't like him very much."

"I gathered that." Jeff took a sip of his tea.

"It's just because they haven't taken the time to get to know him."

Jeff nodded, his gaze thoughtful as he looked into his mug. "How long have you guys been dating?"

"Three years."

Jeff lifted an eyebrow. "That's a long time."

"You've never dated anyone that long?" If her tone was defensive, Jeff didn't appear to react to it.

"If I had," he said, "we'd be married with a child starting to walk and one on the way."

"You want children?"

"I want it all," he sighed, setting down his mug. "A house, a picket fence, a dog. A woman who'll stand by my side. Who's a partner to me. Who has my back and knows I have hers. That's my dream."

It was Saylor's dream too. Though Nick had got impatient when she'd taken him to look at houses. He once shouted at a child who'd spilled a drink on his shoes when they'd gone to the county fair. And he didn't like dogs, or really any animals.

"Scout is pushing me and Brig together," said Jeff.

Saylor's mouth fell open. Then shut. Then opened again. "No, Brig is all wrong for you."

"Who would you suggest?" Jeff's face split into that toothsome grin once more.

Saylor didn't want that sharp smile near any of her sisters. Not because she feared for her sisters' well-being. No, any of them might rip Jeff to pieces. All the men in town knew that to date a Silver sister was to go on a wild ride where they wouldn't have access to the controls.

Except Saylor had never lived up to that

43

reputation. In fact, she'd tried to live it down in her relationship with Nick. But it was her who was left feeling she didn't have the controls of her life in her hands.

Jeff gazed at her, waiting patiently for her answer. "Too bad your hand in marriage isn't on the table. We get along so well."

"Yeah... I mean, right. I mean, Nick said he'd marry me."

"He did?" Jeff's smile lowered a bit, covering the gleam from his teeth.

"Well, he said he'd consider it."

"Yeah?"

"For the ranch."

"Okay."

"But not until all of my other sisters got married first."

Jeff's jaw seemed to harden at those words. Instead of saying anything, he took a sip of his tea. When he finished, he looked her dead in the eye. The smile was back, but this time Saylor swore she saw a predator gleaming in his soft brown eyes.

"Well, he'd better hurry up. A woman like you won't stay single forever. Someone is going to come in and swoop you up when he's not looking."

CHAPTER SIX

*T*he Boyfriend was a lucky man. Not because the scoundrel had a beautiful, kind, trusting woman at his beck and call. Not because the lowlife somehow inspired Saylor's undying devotion. No, the creep was lucky that he wasn't in a combat zone and that Jeff could no longer handle the high-powered rifle he'd favored during his time in service. Otherwise, Jeff would be on an unsanctioned mission tonight.

Instead, Jeff stayed right where he was, on the couch next to Saylor.

"Marriage is a strange thing," Saylor was saying.

"How so?" Jeff asked, placing his empty mug on the wood table.

"Most animals don't mate for life, you know."

Jeff did know. Humans were a part of an elite group of lifeforms on this planet who remained with a partner for more than a reproductive reason. Though the divorce and infidelity rate would decry the notion.

"This animal will," Jeff said, his gaze intent on Saylor.

He could easily see spending the rest of his life with her. Trying to catch that shy smile. Whispering sweet nothings to make those beautiful blue eyes widen. Running his fingers through those lush brown strands and tangled up.

Saylor's hair moved from her shoulder as she turned to face him. Her gaze was wide with surprise. Had she heard his thoughts?

No, she wasn't stunned at the words he hadn't said. She was surprised by the words he had. That angered Jeff. A woman as desirable as Saylor Silver shouldn't be surprised that a man would want to spend the rest of his life with her, and only her.

His left palm tingled, missing the weight of a weapon in his hand. With his right hand, he pressed into his left palm, brushing the thought away. Tamping down on that side of himself.

Growing up in a household of abuse, Jeff had often worried he would do the same to his loved one. When he looked in the mirror, he saw his father's judgmental brown eyes. He knew his mouth pinched in distaste when things didn't go the way he wanted. His hands naturally hung in fists instead of open palms, even at rest.

Jeff knew he had his father inside him. He'd been trained by the General to only let that side out on command. With the General gone, Jeff worked even harder to tamp down his violent nature.

"You're a rare bird, then," Saylor said.

One of her perfectly plucked brows rose. The movement made Jeff think of a bird whose feathers had been ruffled.

"Most birds mate for life. Like swans." Jeff's gaze dipped to Saylor's elegant neck. A picture of two swans linking necks into a heart shape came to mind. The urge to bend his head to hers and kiss her slender neck made his blood pulse.

"Yes, they do." Saylor nodded. "Not ducks, though. Ducks practice seasonal monogamy."

"I don't see why that would matter to a swan, like you."

"Me? A swan?" She giggled. "If anything, I'm an ugly duckling."

Jeff sat up straight, his body poised for retaliation. "Who told you that lie?"

Saylor swallowed. Her body angled away from his. She broke eye contact and shrugged. "No one needed to. I looked in the mirror."

Jeff wasn't sure if she was fishing for a compliment? But he knew she believed what she was saying. Which only served to make him angrier.

He inhaled, bringing in more of her sweet scent. That helped to cool him down. He needed to get himself and his anger under control.

The last thing he wanted was for her to have even an ounce of fear of him. He would never hurt her. His ire was not directed at her. Only at the man who was hurting her even in his absence.

Jeff reached out and took her chin between his fingers. "You're a swan, Saylor. From the long, elegance of your limbs, to the graceful way you move, to the strength with which you carry yourself."

She held still for a long moment. There was something in her eyes, something urgent that wanted to believe him. But then she blinked and turned away.

Jeff wanted to reach out to her, but he knew better. He hadn't known better as a child. So when he reached out to his mother trying to tend to her wounds, she had always brushed him away as though her injuries were nothing. She'd cover them with makeup and was beautiful again in no time. Until her husband's feathers were ruffled again for some new, unpredictable reason. Then the makeup case came out again.

"My dad had three wives," Saylor said. "Technically five because he married my mother three times in total. He always came back to her, even after he went away."

Jeff wasn't sure what Saylor was trying to tell him? But he sensed it was important. So, he listened.

"My mother never took another lover. Because she always knew he would come back. They were each other's first loves. She said you never forget your first love."

And now he understood. The Boyfriend was Saylor's first love. By the looks of him, definitely by his actions, Jeff doubted Nick knew what the word love even meant. So, Jeff doubted Saylor was Nick's first love.

He knew better than to tell her so. When Jeff had tried to tell his own mother that love shouldn't hurt, she had stopped talking to him for weeks.

"I haven't been in love yet," he told her. "But I do believe in forever. When I find that woman, when I find my swan, I'm going to hold her tight forever."

"She's going to be one lucky woman."

"Yes, she will."

Saylor smiled, but the movement didn't reach her eyes. Because her eyes were heavy-lidded. She was clearly tired if the dark bruises under her eyes were any indication.

Jeff kept speaking, keeping his voice low and lulling. Between the hot tea and milk, his voice, and her heavy lids, Saylor was quietly dozing in a matter of minutes.

Jeff lifted his hand to run his fingertips down her temple. The heat that flared throughout his body, including a touch in his numb limb made him know that it wouldn't be the last time he did this. He would fight for the right to hold this swan in his arms for the rest of both of their lives.

CHAPTER SEVEN

*S*aylor was slow to wake. Slow, likely
because it was the best night of sleep
she'd had in days. Maybe weeks. Possibly months.

She hadn't woken a single time during the night
and checked the nightstand's clock to see that the
hour was late and she was still alone. She hadn't
been awoken by the slam of the front door, alerting
her to Nick's arrival back at his apartment only
hours before her day was to begin. She hadn't
awakened to the smell of cheap women's perfume
that she couldn't hold her breath to.

Where Saylor now slept, she inhaled the smell
of cedar and chamomile. She exhaled a sigh of
peace and tranquility. She wasn't alone. She was

wrapped up in a warm embrace. Her head rested against a strong beating heart.

But wait? That couldn't be right. Nick did not like to hold her or be touched when she was beside him.

She often awakened in the night with a chill all over her body as the covers had been yanked off her and wrapped around him. Which was fine as he had low iron, and his blood didn't circulate well, leaving his extremities cold.

Or she woke up disoriented because Nick, if he had come home, was sleeping on the couch with the television blaring.

It all was silent this morning. Because she wasn't at Nick's apartment. She wasn't in her bed. She was on a couch, but the cushions were the softest and warmest Saylor had ever felt. Because the cushions were male flesh.

Saylor lifted her head to find Jeff sleeping peacefully beneath her. She should've scrambled off this man's chest. She should've dashed out of the cabin.

She did neither of those things. She simply stared down at him as he continued to hold her with only one hand pressed to her lower back. She could've easily disentangled herself from his one-armed hold, but her body seized.

She was caught, mesmerized by the peace in his features. Jeff looked almost childlike in his repose. Almost. Jefferson Moore was definitely all male.

That thought unlocked her limbs. Looking at him sleeping peacefully was one thing. Thinking of him as anything other than a friend who'd been there for her during her time of need was something else entirely.

Saylor pressed her hand into the cushion to lift up. When she did, Jeff's arm tightened his hold on her. His fingers dug into the flesh at her low back, as though he didn't want her to go.

Again her limbs locked up, disabling any escape. Saylor had never had a man hold onto her. Nick was always turning away from her. She was always the one to reach out to him, never the other way around.

Nick had never rested his hand at her back. He'd never pulled her to him as though he didn't want her to go. Saylor had to go. Because Jeff wasn't Nick.

Saylor balled her hand into a fist and pushed. As she lifted off Jeff, he sighed. As his lips parted and the small breath escaped, he didn't open his eyes. Neither did he reach for her. He reached for his other arm, the one that hung limp at his side.

It was nippy inside the cabin in the early morning. None of the structures had been built with the modern conveniences of air and heating units. Just the bare necessities.

Saylor covered Jeff with a thick blanket. It was one she'd made when she was younger, when her mother had taught her to crochet. It covered this powerful soldier making him look as though he was covered in down.

Jeff had called her a swan last night. All her life Saylor had felt like an ugly duckling. With an older sister who never tried to be beautiful but still managed it. And a sister who was her twin in age, but her opposite when it came to looks.

Scout and Mareen were swans. Saylor was the duck in the family. Definitely this morning with a rumpled sundress, a rat's nest of hair, and smeared makeup. If Jeff could see her now, he'd see the truth. Which was why she dashed out of the cabin before Jeff could wake up and take in her true state.

When she turned after quietly closing the door, she ran smack dab into Wilson. He reached out to steady her. Once she had her balance, the dark-haired soldier lowered his hands but not his eyebrows. His thoughts were written clearly on his furrowed brows.

"It's not what you think."

Saylor had to pause after saying those words. She had heard them more times than she cared to count coming from her boyfriend's lips. Another reason she should keep giving Nick the benefit of the doubt. What had just transpired between herself and Jeff as they slept in the same space all night was not what Wilson was thinking.

"We were just talking," Scout said.

Wilson said nothing.

"And then, I fell asleep."

Still, Wilson remained mute.

"Nothing happened."

"Wouldn't think so," Wilson finally piped up. "Jefferson is a gentleman."

Saylor's lips pressed together. She wasn't sure if Wilson implied that she wasn't a lady? In any case, the presumption was awful. She finally understood how poor Nick must feel when people made assumptions about him and his behavior.

"You know how his arm injury came about?" Wilson continued. "He saved a kid in our last mission. Grabbed him just before the blast. Jeff was thrown into a wall, shoulder first. The kid walked away without a scratch."

Jeff hadn't told her that. But Saylor could easily

imagine it. He'd stayed up all night with her when he could've shown her to the door, or walked out himself. A woman he barely knew. He hadn't thrown himself over her to protect her from an explosion, but he had let her break down in front of him. Yes, Jefferson was a gentleman.

"But that's Jeff, always putting others before himself, even if he's the one that gets hurt."

The look Wilson gave her was meaningful. Too bad Saylor wasn't clear on his meaning? She wouldn't have the chance to ask him because Wilson turned on his heel and marched away from her.

Saylor didn't have time to ponder the cryptic message the soldier had tried to deliver. She had animals to tend to. So she headed in the other direction to get to work. Before heading inside the house, she grabbed one of the honeysuckles from the bushes at the back of the house.

Tugging at the stamen, she found the prize; a dollop of nectar. It was only a taste. But that's what she was used to getting out of life. And like everything else, she made the most of it.

CHAPTER EIGHT

*J*eff woke. Not with a start. The passage from the dream world to awake was smooth. No nightmares, no sleep paralysis. Just ease. He hadn't woken like this in years.

The lingering scent of honeysuckles filled the air. When he was a kid, there were bushes of the fragrant blooms in his backyard. Whenever things heated up in his household, he'd escape out the back door to the smell of citrus and honey.

It surrounded him now, so strong he could taste it on his tongue. He felt he could reach out and touch it. So he did.

His hand filled with softness. He brought it to his lips, and sure enough, there it was. When he opened his eyes, he saw that he clutched a blanket in his hands.

Looking down at the blanket, he saw a pattern of horses woven into tightly knitted fabrics. At the bottom of the blanket was the name of the garment's creator.

Saylor.

Last night he'd had Saylor in his arms. She had let him in to see her hurts and wounds. She'd trusted him enough to fall asleep in his care. It was a start, but he still cursed himself for falling asleep.

He hadn't intended to. When she'd fallen asleep in his arms last night, he'd been content to look his fill at her heart-shaped face. Saylor had felt more than right in his arms. She'd felt inevitable. There had even been a few instances where Jeff thought he could feel her silky skin against the lifeless fingers of his left hand. Those fingers tingled beneath the warm blanket made by her hands. His right hand clenched with want that she had covered him with her sweet scent before she left him this morning.

Jeff allowed himself one more moment to bask in the heady smell of her. Then he tossed the blanket off, ready to head into battle. Jefferson Moore was ready to report for duty. He had officially signed on to Mission Terminate The Boyfriend.

In his military career, he'd assisted in helping to fell corrupt leadership. He would use those tactics now. But this wouldn't be a simple in and out mission. This would be a coup because Jeff fully intended to install himself as Saylor's new boyfriend. No, not her boyfriend. He wanted to become her husband.

He wouldn't waste three years leading her around. He didn't even want to waste three minutes. The problem was Jeff was sure Saylor had left him this morning to go back to her boyfriend.

Jeff couldn't say that he didn't understand why a woman would go back to a man who neglected her and abused her trust. He'd seen it happen over and over again with his mother. It was lucky for The Boyfriend that the cheater hadn't laid a hand on Saylor. If he ever did, Jeff wouldn't hesitate to take the man down with his good hand tied behind his back.

While showering and dressing for the day, Jeff began to formulate a mission plan in his mind. He'd always been great with maps. He could easily find the best routes on their missions, the ones that kept them out of danger or got them to their location the fastest.

He needed to find a route to Saylor's heart. From

the glimpse he'd gotten last night, he knew the terrain was ravaged and war-torn. He'd have to overcome the treachery Saylor had endured to penetrate all her defenses. Jeff knew exactly where to start.

All cleaned up, Jeff made a beeline for the barn. Even though it was Sunday, there was still work to be done on the ranch. Horses didn't care or even know about weekends. The mares were already out in the pastures munching at the bales of hay laid there.

"Oh, I thought you were Jackson." Brig's posture slumped at the sight of Jeff.

Jeff couldn't help but hide his grin. Brig was trailing after a lost cause. She'd said the Silver sisters had daddy issues. Jackson wasn't old enough to be Brig's father by decades, but the coed was still a touch on the younger side of Jackson's taste.

"I noticed Saylor didn't come home last night," said Brig, her brows drawn together as though in conspiracy with one another. "Last I saw of her, she was headed toward her cabin... where you're staying."

"We were together," Jeff confirmed.

"Dude!" Brig raised her hand in a high five.

"It's not what you think."

"There's something to think about? Yes!"

Jeff tried and failed to hide his grin. There was something to think about. He had to think about how to wedge even more cracks in Saylor's relationship than were already there. And he had to do it before her sisters all married and The Boyfriend had a chance to make good on his promise of marrying Saylor last. Just the thought of putting her last made bile rise in Jeff's throat.

"So, what's the plan?" asked Brig.

The plan was to first get some of the responsibilities off of Saylor's plate. The woman looked like she hadn't rested in weeks. Maybe even months by the heavy circles under her eyes. Jeff wanted to get her well-rested so that she could start to think clearly, see things with fresh eyes. So he was going to step up his assistance around here.

"You finish getting the mares out," he said. "I'll take care of the stallions."

"Are you sure?"

Jeff didn't miss the quick glance Brig shot to his left arm. "I've got this. If I can't help with the horses, she won't even look at me twice."

Brig considered that and then shrugged. She made a clicking sound in her throat, and the two mares she had on leads fell into step with her.

Jeff went into the barn and loosed one of the haystacks. The bale was big and cumbersome. Luckily, it was also a circle, and like a wheel, it just needed a push to gain momentum.

Once four bales were out, he went back for the horses. Thanks to Linc's organizational skills, the tack on the wall was easy to reach. Jeff grabbed a halter. The blond horse, Bingley, was patient as Jeff slid it over the horse's head. The two of them had developed a rapport since Jeff's first day here. But when Jeff made the same sound as Brig for the horse to move forward, Bingley lowered his head.

"It's breakfast time, buddy. You hungry?"

The horse still did not move forward.

Jeff gave a tug on the lead.

Bingley stepped back. He pawed at the ground.

"Easy," Jeff crooned.

Instead of taking it easy, Bingley turned his head. He opened his mouth, and his large teeth bit at his flank.

"I'll bet the hay tastes better than your hide. Come on, fella."

Finally, the horse allowed Jeff to lead him out of the stall. But it was slow going getting the horse to walk forward out of the barn. Jeff was sure once the horse saw the food he'd get with the program. But once they were out of the barn, Bingley still wasn't cooperating.

As they approached the hay, Bingley tugged again on the lead. Before Jeff could get the horse under control, it reared. The movement caught Jeff unawares, and he fell onto his back, just out of reach of the horse's hooves.

Jeff scrambled back as he heard someone shout in the distance. It was Saylor. He'd recognize her voice in a wind tunnel.

He had to get back on his feet. He had to show Saylor that he could manage the horse. But by the time Jeff got to his feet, he looked over to find that the horse was lying on the ground and whining pitifully.

When he looked up, he saw Saylor racing toward him. So much for showing her that he could be a helpmate to her. Shame burned him as he scrambled to his feet. Instead of stopping to check on him, Saylor bypassed Jeff and went directly for the horse.

CHAPTER NINE

"What is it, boy?" Saylor asked Bingley as she came to kneel by the blond Sorrel's head.

In response, Bingley waved his head from side to side. The horse let out a pitiful breath and then laid flat. Saylor had an idea of what was wrong with the horse, but she needed some more information.

"You okay over there?" Saylor asked without looking up at Jeff.

She'd seen the soldier take that fall just before the horse laid itself out on the ground. Saylor had made the calculated move to tend to the horse before tending to the man. Men didn't like it when women noticed any of their weaknesses. She probably shouldn't have even asked Jeff that question. He was sure to go off in a huff, just like Nick did whenever she caught him in a weak moment.

The thought of Jeff walking off in a huff made Saylor incredibly sad. The idea of him huffing seemed wrong in her mind. It belied that even demeanor of his. But she knew that all men had tempers, and she couldn't deal with the man's tantrum right now. She had a sick horse to tend to.

"What do you need me to do?"

Saylor glanced up. She was sure there was utter shock in her gaze.

Jeff was back on his feet. He was standing close to her, but not too close. Just close enough to her to swoop in if she needed. But far back enough as though he trusted her to handle this matter.

What did she need him to do? Had she heard that right? Not *It wasn't my fault.* Or *You should've known what would happen*. Was Jeff trying to be of assistance?

It was a sight Saylor had never seen before. She had to blink a few times to be sure she wasn't hallucinating. Then she had to clear her throat before her words were intelligible.

"Just tell me what was going on before he dropped," she finally managed.

"I was leading him out of the barn to have his meal," said Jeff. "He was antsy in his stall. He kept turning his head when I tried to put on his halter. But I knew he had to be hungry since he kept biting at his flank."

That confirmed what Saylor had been thinking. "It's likely colic."

"Colic?" Jeff said. "Like a baby?"

"Something like that." Saylor managed to bring the horse back to standing. "It's a bad tummy ache. Eating is probably the last thing he wants to do."

She ran her hand over the horse's side. Leaning in, she pressed her ear to his belly to listen. Sure enough, she heard the grumbling there.

"What's there to do?" asked Jeff.

"It doesn't sound like a serious case, just a mild bout. So, I'm going to work his pressure points first."

Saylor was already moving into position. She reached down the horse's leg, squeezing at the spot above his hoof. She rotated the joint she found there, giving it a good amount of direct pressure.

Bingley looked back at her. The horse let out a low whine that sounded like a sigh of relief.

"There, there," she said. "It's already getting better, isn't it?"

"Should I hold him still? He could kick you."

Jeff was just behind her. She felt the sigh of heat from his breath against the cone of her ear. She almost shivered. What made her warm through was the worry and protectiveness in Jeff's voice.

"He's not gonna kick," she said, her voice a low and rumbly ache like the sounds coming from Bingley's belly. "This is helping it feel better. So, he'll hold still."

Saylor couldn't hold still with Jeff beside her. There was a part of her that wanted to turn around and find her way back into that space at the center of his chest. That space where she had found her own relief just hours ago. An ache rose low in her stomach.

"Have you eaten this morning?" Jeff asked.

Saylor flushed that he'd heard her want. "I will. Once I finish soothing Bingley."

"You have a habit of doing that."

"Doing what?"

"Putting others before you."

Saylor frowned at that. "Well, this poor horse can't soothe himself."

"I could take over if you showed me what to do. Then you could go grab a bite to eat."

What was he trying to say? That she was too thin? Too fat? Saylor wasn't sure where the dig on her was coming from, so she rounded the horse and went to his tail.

"Let me give you a hand," said Jeff.

"I'll need two hands for this part." The moment the words were out of her mouth, Saylor grimaced. "That's not what I meant."

She turned to Jeff, expecting anger, or at least withdrawal. There was neither on his face. He stood by her, steady and calm.

Saylor was anything but. Her fingers shook as she grasped the strands of Bingley's tail. There were some of his vertebrae in the hair there. Saylor pulled down on it with tight pressure.

All the while, she watched the horse. The horse watched her. Jeff watched them both, but she noticed that Jeff's gaze lingered mostly on her.

She must still look a fright. She had just hopped out of the shower. She hadn't had time to put on any makeup or fix her hair.

"He didn't hurt you, did he?" she asked.

"No," said Jeff. "I thought I was helping."

"No, you were. You did. How were you to know Bingley was sick?"

"Yeah, I guess."

"Listen, about last night...I'm so sorry for overstaying my welcome and falling asleep on you like I did. And then waking up and leaving without saying goodbye."

The words all came out in a huge gush. They weren't the only thing that came out in a gush. Saylor let go of Bingley's tale just in time. She only just managed to leap out of the way as the horse dropped proof that his belly was starting to feel better.

Before Saylor could wobble, she was encased in a strong arm. A strong arm that felt familiar. Jeff had one arm around her, but she felt engulfed by him.

"You don't have to apologize for anything," he said. "I'm here for you, whatever you need."

Saylor couldn't take her gaze from his mouth. Or the words he'd just said. As Jeff held her to his chest, her own belly stopped its grumbling as she let out a sigh of contented relief.

"Morning," called Brig.

As though she'd been caught, Saylor sprung herself out of Jeff's arms. She felt the instant loss of his warmth. Her insides went to mush. Or rather, that was how her foot felt as she stepped right into Bingley's heaping gift of wellness.

That was also the moment her cell phone decided to ring.

CHAPTER TEN

*J*eff watched as Saylor slipped out of his hold. It wasn't a hard thing to do as one arm hung uselessly at his side. If it had been working, he might've been able to lock her down. Instead, she was sliding her boots against the grass, trying to remove as much manure as possible as she answered her cell phone.

He knew without seeing the caller ID who was on the other end of that line. The Boyfriend. *She keeps going back to him*, her sister had said. Well, Jeff was here to interrupt that script. He just had to figure out how.

"Looks like you're making progress." Brig grinned at him from the fencing. With ease, the young woman hopped over the fence, deftly avoiding the little gifts dropped by the horse. Bingley was up and moving about once more. He came to Brig, lowering his head for a pat.

"Aw, did you have a bellyache, Bingley Wingley?" crooned Brig.

Jeff's attention couldn't be moved from Saylor. She moved farther away from him, away from the barn, and farther out to pasture. He couldn't hear what she was saying, but he saw that she wasn't smiling as she talked on the phone.

Was Nick saying something to upset her? Was the man she had chosen taking another crack at her?

Jeff hadn't missed Nick's disparaging remarks about her at the reception, as The Boyfriend prepared to leave with not one but two other women. Neither had Jeff missed the slight fall of Saylor's smile. That dip in her perfect lips had appeared to Jeff an avalanche of hurt.

Jeff felt a tingle in his left hand. Was it a tingle to cuff Nick? Or a tingle to reach for Saylor. He knew that if given the chance, he would choose comforting Saylor. But he was already having a hard time getting her to accept his care. It was clear she was unused to a man looking after her.

"I saw you two in what looked like a pretty intimate moment," said Brig.

"She came into my arms to avoid falling into manure," Jeff said.

"If that isn't a metaphor, then I don't know what is." Brig sent Bingley off into the round pen with a pat on the rear. The horse walked on, still ignoring the hay that Jeff had laid out.

"Nick was the first guy to tell Saylor she was pretty."

"The first guy? You can't be serious. She's gorgeous."

"I know. But she doesn't believe that. You haven't seen Mareen. Saylor and Mareen are the same age, just a few months apart. Irish twins."

Jeff frowned at the term. The General had told his men that he'd come from a Germanic heritage.

"My mom found out she was pregnant on the day of my dad's wedding to Mareen's mom, Catherine the Cruel."

Jeff cringed. He'd had no idea what a soap opera the general's life had been outside of the military. The man ran everything by the book. His movements were precise and regimented. But Jeff knew all too well that love was a messy affair.

His father had heated on his mom numerous

times. Cheated wasn't the best word. It implied a trick or dishonesty. Patrick Moore had no problems telling his wife the truth, and watching the pain crease her features.

And still, Audrey Moore had stayed with her sadistic husband. Stayed to endure the harsh words, brutal caresses, and the constant infidelity.

Jeff had heard Nick's harsh words to Saylor. He suspected the man was relaying more to her over a cell tower. Jeff also suspected the infidelity. But he'd seen Saylor physically turn away from potential evidence the other night.

"I've tried everything I can think of to break the two of them up," Brig was saying.

When he was a teen, Jeff had tried everything he could think of to get his mother to leave. He'd shown her evidence of the cheating, but she had only turned away. He'd run away, but she hadn't followed. He'd shouted that his father would be the death of her, but she'd turned up the sound on the television.

"Telling her he's a worthless scumbag doesn't work," Brig was saying. "She just makes excuses for him. I've tried spreading gossip so that it reaches her ears through others. But everyone knows how he is. I've even tried throwing his ex-girlfriends at him, like at the wedding."

"That was you?"

"Yup, I invited them. And the idiot took the bait. Problem is, Saylor didn't let him off the hook."

That indeed was the problem. Again, Jeff got that fleeting feeling in the palm of his hand, an itching feeling that made him want to ball his fist. But when he looked down, his fingers hung limply at his side.

"His exes will dance and dally with him," Brig continued. "But none of them want to keep him. Surprisingly, they're actually smart. If total dishonest, traitors to their gender."

Jeff's father was the same. The women he brought into his life had no shame as they pranced on his arm for a few days or weeks. They allowed him to drip them in cheap jewels and two-star restaurant meals while his family scraped by. But none of them wanted to stay with a man who had a wife and child.

"My old college roommate befriended her bestie's cheating boyfriend and then sabotaged him from the other side," Brig said with a gleam to her blue eyes. "It was the most brilliant espionage I've ever witnessed. Too bad I can't pull that off in this case. I tried to have a pleasant conversation with The Boyfriend, but it turned my stomach."

"I could do that." It was a tactic Jeff had never tried when he was trying to split his parents up. Mainly because he'd been far too young to manage or even consider it.

"Yeah?" said Brig.

"Infiltrate behind enemy lines? I've done it before."

That had been part of his job in the military, turning assets against the bad guys. It was intel he'd gathered that led them to their last mission. The intel had been good. They'd gotten the bad guy and saved many lives. Even though they'd lost the one life they held dear.

It would be nothing to Jeff to befriend this particular enemy if only to take Nick down and save this most precious asset. He owed it to the general, he told himself. But it was his heart that was in charge of this particular decision.

His mother had chosen time and again to stay with his father. But Jeff was determined to rescue Saylor from this particular villain. Even if Jeff didn't wind up the hero.

"I have to go into the city," Saylor said as she walked back to them.

"What does he need now?" asked Brig. "His pancakes cut in bite-sized pieces?"

"That wasn't Nick." Saylor scowled at her sister. "It was his dry cleaner. They're closing up early and wanted him to pick up his suit. He's not answering his phone, so they called me."

"You're going to run all the way to town to pick up his dry cleaning?" said Brig, lifting an eyebrow.

"But Nick still has my car," Saylor said as though she hadn't heard her sister or seen the raised brow of disbelief.

"He always has your car," Brig murmured.

"I'll drive you," said Jeff.

Saylor blinked up at him. Then she shook her head. "You don't have to do that."

"I need to pick up some things anyway." The lie was smooth coming from Jeff's lips. He'd twisted more flimsy truths to get people to turn on corrupt leaders. "You'd do me a favor by providing the company."

"If you're sure I'm not putting you out?"

Jeff offered Saylor a pleasant grin in answer. The only person he was focused on putting out was that boyfriend of hers. As he and Saylor walked off, Jeff turned back to Brig, who winked at him, throwing two large thumbs up.

The plan was in motion.

CHAPTER ELEVEN

*S*aylor pulled the strands of her hair back and away from her face. She chided herself for letting her hair down for so long. Scout had insisted that her younger sister let her tresses flow free yesterday, and Saylor had acquiesced because she knew better than to argue with a bride on her wedding day.

Now, she gathered the strands into a tight queue at the back of her head. Nick often told her with her hair down, it made her face look fat. Pleasing her sister for one day was fine. Now Saylor was back to her normal routine, and at the top of that routine was being pleasing to the eyes of her boyfriend.

Although with her hair now in its customary ponytail, she was uncomfortable sitting in the passenger seat. She turned her head left, then right, trying to find the best angle on the headrest.

"Is my driving making you nervous?" asked Jeff.

Saylor glanced up and at his profile. His gaze was on the road, but she could feel all of his attention on her. She'd never had someone focus like this on her. Well, she'd never had a man focus so much of his attention on her.

"I do still have a driver's license," he said when she didn't answer. "I was cleared by the DMV to drive even though one-handed."

Now Saylor's glance fell down to the hand he held in his lap. His left hand was caught up in its sling as his right hand maneuvered on the steering wheel. Saylor blushed again to be caught staring so openly at the man's lap.

"I'm not clear to operate military-grade heavy equipment, but I can manage a car."

"I wasn't thinking about your abilities," she said. "I know you're perfectly capable. I trust that you wouldn't do anything to put me in danger."

"You do?" he said, a note of disbelief in his voice.

With that note of uncertainty, she thought she should be nervous. But she wasn't. The week she'd known Jefferson Moore, he had shown at every turn that he was an able-bodied man despite his injury.

Even after the mishap this morning with Bingley, Jeff hadn't shied away from doing what had to be done.

Their gazes locked as they ambled down the deserted road that led to town. Jeff's light brown eyes skated from her eyes to her hairline.

"What?" Saylor asked, patting at her hair, searching for any wayward strands that may have escaped her elastic band.

"Nothing," he said in that tone that belied there was something. "It's just, you look different with your hair up."

Saylor's fingers trailed down the mane of hair that hung over her shoulder. "Nick likes it up."

From the corner of her eye, she saw Jeff's jaw tense. She braced herself for a crack about her boyfriend. Nick didn't have many guy friends. In fact, he didn't have any. It was because he was so misunderstood, was all.

"Nick's a lucky guy," said Jeff. "To have a woman who is beautiful no matter her hairstyle."

Saylor could only stare. She felt a tendril escape her ponytail at the back. She did not reach to press the loose strand back into place.

Jeff glanced at her again, this time flashing her that genial smile he had last night when he'd asked her to stay for warm tea. He should've had his eyes on the road. She should've felt unsafe. But the truth was, this man made her feel safe. Why else would she spend the night in his arms?

Her cheeks heated at the thought of last night. She waited for the guilt, for the shame to assault her. It never came.

Saylor's mind thought back to waking up in Jeff's arms. She'd never felt such peace as in those few moments. The residual peace left no room for guilt or shame.

Nick never held her. He rarely hugged her. Wait? Had he ever embraced her with the intention to offer comfort?

She and Jeff were cruising down the main street now. Honor Valley had a colonial feel to it, with red brick shops lining the street. Wooden placards hung over doors announcing the family name first and then the type of business.

"It's just over there." Saylor pointed to Cohen's Dry Cleaner's Shop.

The Cohens had already put up a closed for business sign. Everyone knew their oldest granddaughter was expecting her first child. They had announced they would be closing for a couple of weeks at the beginning of the month to be there for the happy occasion. Though it was Nick's dry cleaning she was picking up, a pang of guilt still washed over Saylor that she was holding them up. She should've anticipated this.

Jeff parked the car in front of the shop. Before he could unfasten his seat belt, Saylor stopped him.

"Don't trouble yourself," she said. "I'll just run in and get it."

"I'm going to get out to open your door for you."

"I can open my own door, Jeff." She grinned, pleased by the old world chivalry at the same time that she was unsure what to do with it. "I mean, I know you can open it for me. But there's no need to—"

"Saylor?"

"Yes, Jeff?"

"Stay where you are," he said pointedly. "I'll be around to open your door like the gentleman your father trained me to be."

Saylor pressed her back into the seat. The place at the back of her head where her ponytail was gathered found the right spot at that moment.

Jeff undid his seatbelt and opened the door. He walked around the truck with sure strides. He arrived at the passenger door and pulled the door open wide. Then reached for her.

Saylor reached for his hand, but she was held back. She'd forgotten to take off her own seat belt. Seeing the problem, Jeff reached across her body.

That peace that had lulled her to sleep in another man's arms woke inside her. But it was no longer calm and quiet. The head of it seemed to perk up, look around, and settle on Jeff. As it did so, heat bloomed somewhere in Saylor's middle, making her breath catch.

Jeff lifted his head. They were eye to eye, only a few inches apart. She could lean forward and be right back in that space at the center of his chest. There was a part of her, the warm awakened part, that wanted to reach for that spot.

A click cut through the imagined tension she felt. The strap let her go, giving her the space to move. Saylor hesitated.

Jeff backed up, giving her the space she needed to climb out of the car. In the gulf between them, he held out his hand once more. Saylor had to take a breath to regain her composure. Her fingers trembled as she put her hand in his. The instant she felt the coolness of his palm, her fingers stopped shaking.

Jeff wrapped his fingers around hers. And there

it was again, that feeling of safety and peace. Only it was a few degrees warmer now.

"You good?" asked Jeff.

Yes, she was good. She had never felt so good. She felt so good that she didn't let go of Jeff's hand as they walked into the shop to pick up her boyfriend's dry cleaning.

CHAPTER TWELVE

*S*aylor's hand in his felt good. It felt right. It felt perfect.

Jeff had lied to her earlier before he'd climbed out of the car to come around and hand her out. A gentleman would not be holding the hand of an unavailable woman. A gentleman would keep his distance.

Jeff was not a gentleman.

General Silver may have chastised the men when it came to their manners. But the man had also trained them to be merciless when it came to winning battles. This wasn't a battle Jeff was fighting. He was waging full out war.

It was a war for Saylor's heart, and Jeff was all in.

He was prepared to use any and all tactics to press his advantage. So far, he wasn't meeting with any resistance.

Part of Jeff knew that that was because his target had never received an actual full-court press. He doubted Nick had ever had to press his suit at all. It was written all over her face. And it was criminal.

Jeff wanted to pummel The Boyfriend for the neglect. But had Nick not neglected Saylor, then it would've been all the more harder for Jeff to move forward with this sneak attack.

Walking a few steps away from the car, Jeff reveled in the feel of Saylor at his side. There was space between them, but he knew that if he pulled her closer, she'd fit right into his side. He already knew that she fit against his chest like a puzzle piece he'd been searching for all his life.

Jeff was sure no one else would fit his hard edges as smoothly as Saylor Silver. Which was why this wasn't a game for him. He was in this to win it.

He rubbed the back of her knuckles lightly as they walked into the dry cleaner's shop. The bell overhead dinged as if to signal that this round was up. Saylor was here to collect her boyfriend's things. However, Jeff didn't let go of Saylor's hand. And she didn't tug free of his hold.

"Thank you for coming in, you two," said the small woman behind the counter. She had a cloud of gray hair and the type of crow's feet at the corners of her eyes and mouth, the kind that told she was prone to laughing and smiling a lot. Which made it odd that a second later, she was frowning.

"Oh?" The woman, who Jeff assumed was Mrs. Cohen, looked between them at their clasped hands. "I didn't realize you had a new beau, Saylor. I wouldn't have called you for Nick's things if I had known."

That's when Saylor dropped Jeff's hand. It took everything in him to let her go. She even stepped away from him, putting a foot of distance between them. Instead of stepping forward and back into her personal space, Jeff decided to keep sentry at her back.

"Oh no, Jeff isn't my beau. He's my..."

Jeff's blood heated that Saylor hesitated on their relationship status. The word *friend* should've rolled off her tongue with ease. Could that pause mean that she was already warming up to the idea that they could be more?

He wanted to wait until Saylor filled in that blank. Instead, he dipped his head to the woman in greeting. "Jefferson Moore, ma'am. Pleased to meet you."

"Such nice manners," said Mrs. Cohen. "I always said you could do better than Nick Murphy. No one thought he was good enough for you."

Saylor's cheeks heated. Her head lowered as she spoke. "I'm still with Nick, Mrs. Cohen."

"Oh." That oh was not a sound made in embarrassment. It was not a question mark as though Mrs. Cohen had misheard. It was the sound of weary disappointment.

"Jeff just gave me a ride," said Saylor. "I'll just grab Nick's things and get out of your way so you can get out of here and see your great-grandbaby."

Mrs. Cohen nodded and disappeared around a divider. "I wasn't able to get the lipstick stain off the collar. It was a pretty dark shade of red."

From his vantage point behind her, Jeff saw Saylor's shoulders tense. He balled his right hand in a fist, aching to step forward and soothe her. Again there was that tingle in his left palm, as though it wanted a part in the war effort.

Mrs. Cohen came from behind the divider with a plastic bag in one hand and a scrap of paper in the other. "I found this in the back pants pocket. There's a phone number on it. It looked important, so I kept it."

The woman's face was impassive, but Jeff saw the challenge there. Unfortunately, Saylor didn't rise to the occasion. Her face was implacable. But Jeff saw cracks. Fine little fissures that he knew he could use against Nick. But he hesitated.

Jeff had gathered mountains of evidence against his father's infidelity. And still, his mother never left. Not for any of the lipstick stains she'd laundered herself. Not for the blocked numbers that called their residence. Not for the couple of women who showed up at her doorstep.

Audrey Moore had not left her husband. She had not strayed from her vows. Not the times her husband raised a hand to her for insinuating that he'd done something wrong.

Jeff had held his mother's hand many a night. He'd tended to the wounds both internal and external. But every time he tried to tug her away, she would not budge. In the end, it was Jeff who'd left.

Leaving his mother behind had devastated him. Even to this day, he still held out hope that one day she would leave. Looking at Saylor's stiff upper lip, Jeff knew he could not walk away from her.

"I gather you're settling Nick's bill for the month as well, dear?" asked Mrs. Cohen.

"Of course." Saylor reached for her pocketbook. After a few moments of rummaging through the bag, her cheeks were even redder than the lipstick stain. "I left my wallet at the ranch."

"Don't worry," said Jeff. "I'll get it."

For the first time that he'd known her, Jeff saw Saylor's brows raise in alarm. "You don't have..."

But Jeff ignored her protests. He exchanged a look with Mrs. Cohen. It was the same look that Brig gave him when they were concocting a plan to break the couple up. It appeared everyone had that look when it came to Saylor and The Boyfriend. Clearly, Mrs. Cohen wanted him gone as much as the other Silver sisters.

Jeff winked at her after she handed him the receipt. Mrs. Cohen gave him an encouraging smile, a smile that said bring out the heavy weaponry if you have to. Jeff intended to.

"I'm sorry about that," said Saylor once they were out of the store. "I'll pay you back."

"Don't worry about it," said Jeff. "I'm sure Nick would do the same for me if I forgot my wallet."

Saylor chewed at her lower lip, not meeting Jeff's

gaze. "Well, thank you again for the ride. I can walk to Nick's apartment from here."

"Not on my watch. I'll deliver you safely to your destination."

Jeff held out his hand for her. Her moment's hesitation was only a second this time. Saylor took his hand as he helped her into the car. But her eyes weren't on him. They were on the faint stain of red on the collar of her boyfriend's suit.

CHAPTER THIRTEEN

*B*efore getting into the car, Saylor let the slip of paper found in Nick's suit fall to the ground. She should feel guilty over littering, but she doubted anyone would pay much mind to the scrap. The slip of paper was no longer with her, but the numbers were burned into her mind. Because Saylor knew to whom that sequence of numbers belonged.

Holly Marks had given Saylor her number once in middle school when they'd been paired up on a class project. Holly had been the most popular girl all throughout middle and high school. Next to Mareen, of course. But unlike Mareen, who had never wanted the attention her good looks brought, Holly wanted all eyes on her at all times.

She got the attention she craved because of her on-again, off-again, tumultuous gossip-worthy relationship with Nick. Their arguments in the lunchroom were the stuff of legend. Their makeup make-out sessions behind the bleachers were more instructive than the Judy Blume novels in the library. Nick would often emerge with Holly's devil-red lipstick stained on his lips and shirt collar.

They were forever breaking up, dating each others' friends, getting back together again, only to break up again. It was dizzying to pay attention to. Saylor had followed every twist and turn of the high school drama.

By the time high school was over, so were Nick and Holly. Or so she had thought.

"Where do you want to go, Saylor?"

The sound of Jeff's voice brought her back to the present. His voice was gentle but strong. Coaxing, yet insistent.

Saylor wanted to wrap herself up in the warm comfort of Jeff's voice. No, she wanted to wrap herself up in his arms and not deal with any of the past protruding into her present. Not the phone number. Not the red shade of lipstick Holly Marks had been wearing at the wedding yesterday.

Even though she closed her eyes, Saylor still

couldn't block any of it out. She just wanted the world to stop for a moment. And then it did.

A large hand came to rest on her knee. That hand grounded her. It gave her an ounce of strength. She just wasn't sure what to do with the boost of power.

"Tell me what you need?"

Saylor wanted to laugh. She had no idea what she needed. She had been so busy tending to the needs of others that it never occurred to her that she might have any of her own.

What Saylor needed was just to sit still at this moment with this man who gave her strength, who gave her peace, and asked nothing of her in return. Jeff had driven a few blocks down. The next block over was Nick's apartment building.

Saylor turned from the brownstone and faced Jeff. She expected to see pity on the handsome soldier's features. Jeff had to be thinking the worst of Nick. If she were honest with herself, she'd admit she was more concerned with what Jeff was thinking of her.

"The phone number belongs to his first girlfriend. She was at the wedding."

Jeff said nothing. He only turned his torso in the

driver's seat and waited. His gaze landed softly on her with not a single ounce of judgment.

She had a boyfriend with a wandering eye. All men had wandering eyes. Look at her father. But even with Abe Silver's wandering eye, he always came back to his first wife. Holly had been back in town for over two years now, but Nick hadn't dumped Saylor to get back together with her. Though Saylor had seen this shade of lipstick on more than one of his shirt collars recently.

Her gaze couldn't hold Jeff's. Her head dipped, and her eyes fell on Jeff's collar. There were no stains there from a woman's cosmetics. When she looked back up, Jeff's eyes weren't wandering. They were fixed on her. Like there was no one else in the world. Like he had nothing to do but sit here with his hand on her knee, grounding her into a reality she wasn't sure she was ready to face.

"You love him."

Saylor wasn't sure if she heard a question mark on the end of Jeff's statement? Or a period? So she wasn't sure how to respond.

"I'm going to drop his suit off," she said in response.

Jeff didn't argue with her. He simply nodded. Then he reached for the driver's side door.

"No, you don't have to come with me."

He turned back, his gaze now hard. "Didn't we already establish this? I am a gentleman. A gentleman always opens the door for a lady. You're the lady in this scenario."

Saylor sat obediently while she waited for Jeff to round the car. She looked down at the suit in her lap. That red lipstick stain glared back at her, accusingly.

As though she were the one who had done something wrong. Obviously, she had. If she couldn't keep her boyfriend satisfied.

It wasn't the first time she'd seen lipstick stains on his clothing, in a different shade. There had been business cards and napkins with scribbled numbers in his pockets before. Random texts, a little too personal to be work-related, popped up on his cell phone at late hours in the night when he left it unguarded.

Day in and day out, Saylor had tried to push those memories aside. When they wouldn't go, she would try to explain them away. All her excuses flew out of the window as Jeff opened the passenger door.

Jeff held his hand out to her. Saylor took the offered hand and immediately felt grounded again.

None of the thoughts surrounding her boyfriend's infidelity plagued her as Jeff's fingers gripped hers. Saylor didn't want to let go. So she didn't.

She allowed Jeff to hold her hand as they walked around to the front of Nick's apartment building. She didn't let go as they climbed the stairs together, side by side, to the second floor. She didn't let go until she had to fumble with the keys to the front door.

"Thanks for the ride," she said.

Jeff's right arm tensed beside her. "You sure you want to stay here? I could wait and drive you back to the ranch."

It was a simple question. All it needed was a yes or no answer. Somehow it wasn't so simple.

Did she want to stay here with her boyfriend and his lipstick-stained clothing?

Did she want to go back to the ranch with Jeff, who would open the door for her and leave her feeling grounded and peaceful?

The key was in the door. Her fingers turned it as she turned to Jeff to give him an answer. The door should've opened with her movement. It did, just a bit. Until the top chain stopped her entry.

Inside Saylor heard muffled voices. One of the voices was low and masculine. The other high and feminine. At the sound of the chain stopping the door's opening, the voices stopped.

Again Saylor closed her eyes, trying to shut out the world. She wanted to use her body to block Jeff's vision, his hearing. She didn't want him to see this.

From the crack in the door, Nick appeared. He was in boxers that were askew. His hair was mussed. "Saylor? What are you doing here?"

Saylor stepped back from the door, letting it shut in her face. It was a childish move. She knew Nick had seen her. When she stepped back, she stepped right against Jeff's chest. The urge to turn her head and bury her face there was overwhelming.

The chain rattled at the door. It flung open and Nick appeared. The guilty look on his face rearranged itself when he saw Jeff. "What's going on here?"

Nick reached for her. Instead of going to him, like she always did, she handed him his dry cleaning.

"I'm sorry," Saylor said. "But they couldn't get Holly's lipstick stain out."

Nick blanched at Holly's name on Saylor's lips. Then a bright color, similar to the shade of lipstick still staining his shirt, warmed his cheeks. Nick's lips sputtered a few times before coherent words formed.

"What are you talking about? I haven't seen her since..."

"Last night at the wedding," Saylor supplied. "When you two left together to catch up."

"Right," he agreed. "So, this couldn't be hers."

"Kellie's, maybe?"

Nick cocked his head, as though in thought. He realized his mistake a few seconds too late. When he opened his mouth again, a bump sounded from the bedroom.

"A book must've fallen," said Nick.

Saylor nodded. Something had fallen. The scales from her eyes.

"You were never going to marry me, were you?" she said.

"Is that what this is about?" He sounded relieved. As though she hadn't just caught him red-collared for the umpteenth time. As though she wasn't aware that there was someone else in the apartment. As though she was going to come back into his arms again, pretending that he'd done nothing wrong.

That's when Saylor realized. Nick never came back to her. He was always flitting off to flirt and step outside of their relationship. It was Saylor who always came back to him.

"I'm never going to be enough for you, am I?" she said.

Nick's gaze cut from Saylor to Jeff, who still stood firm at her back. "Exactly what's going on here? You stepping out on me with this cripple?"

Saylor expected Jeff to lash out. Another man would have. Jeff was no ordinary man. Instead of lashing out at Nick, Jeff wrapped his strong arm around Saylor and pulled her against him. It was that last ounce of strength she needed to do what she had to do.

It was the hardest thing she had to do, but Saylor stepped out of Jeff's embrace. She stepped toward Nick. With her foot just over the threshold of the apartment, she reached around to the wall until she felt what she was looking for; her car keys.

Without another word, she turned on her heel and walked away.

CHAPTER FOURTEEN

The moment Saylor stepped away from him, Jeff wanted to pull her back into his embrace. It was enough to watch her walk away from the cheat standing in the door. He had to quickstep it to keep up with her now.

Saylor tore down the stairs and flew out the door of the apartment building. Jeff wasn't surprised to see that The Boyfriend didn't follow behind her. He didn't even call out to her.

Was he The Ex-Boyfriend now? He had to be. She'd caught him red-handed. Red lip-sticked. Red-penned phone numbered. And red boxer shorted.

Though Jeff was sure this couldn't have been the first time. It just so happened that this was the time she wasn't making any excuses for him. This was the time she'd had enough.

The analytical part of Jeff wanted to stop Saylor and ask what had changed? He needed to know so that he could keep those parameters engaged. Brig had said Saylor always went back to Nick. Jeff wouldn't have been able to stand by in that hallway if she'd stepped through that apartment door and gone back to a man who would treat her so callously.

If Saylor hadn't been running away from him, Jeff would've stayed behind and given the cheater a piece of his mind using his fist. Nick was lucky Jeff was only working with one arm. Otherwise, it would be a bloodbath.

That thought made Jeff slow his pace. Ever since he'd joined the military, he'd slowly gained control over the anger that lived inside of him. The part of him that had come from his father. He never attacked without orders.

He had no orders to attack anyone. His final order from the general had been to protect his daughters. Jeff wouldn't want to disappoint the man who had given him so much. With a deep calming breath, Jeff pushed the anger and frustration he wanted to direct at Nick out of his body until none of it was left.

When he finally caught up to Saylor, she stood staring at a car. Looking into the driver's side, Jeff could see what she was staring at. A woman's jacket was casually slung on the passenger seat. It was the same shade of red as the stain on the suit from the dry cleaners.

"I can't drive," she said, not looking at him. "Can you take me home, please?"

"Of course."

He expected her to move away from his touch. She didn't. She allowed him to guide her back to his vehicle. There was tension in her walk, in the way she held her shoulders, in the way she looked blankly at the world around her.

Jeff handed her inside the truck. She sat looking out the window, her eyes unfocused. He reached across her and pulled her seat belt on. The click of the buckle into its slot roused her. Their gazes locked.

The light blue of Saylor Silver's eyes darkened. The circles beneath her lids had grown heavier on the short walk. Her lower lip trembled.

"You think I'm stupid, don't you?" she asked.

"No," Jeff said, holding her heavy gaze and not flinching from the weight of it. "Not even slightly."

Jeff did not move his hand from the seat belt's lock. He held it in place. He hadn't been able to get his mother to leave his father, but he was sure he would not allow Saylor any space or quarter to go back up those stairs.

"I think you're one of the smartest women I have ever met. You are trusting and filled with optimism. You simply misplaced your loyalty. It happens."

Saylor winced. At the crinkle of her eyelids, tears pricked at the corners. Jeff ached to rub his fingers there. To capture all of her hurts and take them away.

And so he did. He lifted his hand from the belt to her face. He caught the tears before they could fall and leave any trace.

"My mom stayed with my dad, even after he beat her," he confessed.

Jeff had never admitted that to anyone. The general had guessed. But Jeff had never confirmed it.

Saylor's next tears didn't fall. They stayed at the edge of her eyelids as she peered down at him. Jeff didn't remove his hand from her face, just in case. He didn't want her to cry for him. He wanted to bring her joy. He also wanted her to understand that he knew her pain.

"She stayed and took all of his anger, his frustrations, his shame. She stayed until he raised his hand to me."

Saylor closed her eyes in relief. He hated to tell her that that wasn't the end of the story. So, he pushed on.

"When I joined the military, she went back to him."

Saylor's eyes flashed open. "Did he...? Had he changed?"

"For a while. But old habits..."

"Nick never..."

"Even if the abuse isn't physical, it still scars."

Pain crumpled her features. Jeff brought her into his arms. He held her as the tears left her. He held her as he tried in vain to soak up every ounce of hurt this woman had ever felt. He felt the phantom ache in his left arm that wanted to press her more fully to him.

"What am I going to do?"

It was a whisper, so he almost didn't hear it. He pulled back slightly, not letting her go so that he could look into her face as she spoke.

"We're going to lose the ranch because of me,"

Saylor sniffled. "Scout's married. Mareen will be married soon. Tilly's got prospects. I know Scout is trying to pair you and Brig. And Gunny—" Saylor let out a humorless chuckle. "She won't have any problems getting a guy to marry her. People tend to do what she tells them. But what about me?"

With the humor gone, Saylor sniffled again. Her beautiful features crumpled into a mask of misery. Her head fell, but Jeff's hands were there, not letting her get too down on herself.

"What do you mean, what about you?" he said.

"No other man besides Nick has ever shown interest in me. And now my only prospect—"

"He was not your only prospect," said Jeff. "And I highly doubt no other man has ever shown interest in you. You must not be paying close attention."

Her head tilted back under her own strength. Those blue eyes brightened hesitantly, as though there were more clouds just outside her vision.

"You're beautiful, Saylor. I told you before, you're a swan. Not the duckling you pretend to be."

Jeff held still as Saylor searched his gaze. The clouds still threatened in the blue, but he saw a small ray of hope.

"Jefferson?"

"Yes, Saylor?"

"I know Scout thinks you and Brig are a match, but..."

"Brig and I don't think we're a match."

"You don't?" Saylor's brows lifted. All traces of clouds fled. "Do you think... Would you consider marrying me? Not for real, of course. Just so we could save the ranch. I wouldn't make any demands. You could still date and live on the ranch and—"

"Saylor?"

She closed her eyes and took a deep breath. "I'm sorry for asking. It was a stupid idea—"

"I'll marry you."

Her eyes flashed open. "You will?"

"It would be my honor."

It would be more than honor. It would be more than duty. Jeff's new mission was clear. For the rest of his days, he would show this woman what it meant to be cherished.

CHAPTER FIFTEEN

"You said yes?"

Saylor opened her mouth to respond to her older sister. But the words caught in her throat as she looked down at the spice rack. She picked up the glass jar that held the vanilla, only to see that it was an imitation of the seasoning rather than the real thing.

During the lean times, their mother had begun buying bargain brands of everything. Dollar Store seasonings that often had a grain of sand in the salt. A peppermill that only had a few good cranks in it before the peppercorns spilled out.

It was no longer a lean time in the Silver household. Saylor and her sisters had turned the ranch around. They were making a profit off the rehab of racehorses, the veterinarian care Saylor gave to the surrounding ranches, and the lessons Tilly gave. Even Gunny's research on rare horse breeds brought in money for the ranch. All meaning there was no need for the fake stuff on the spice rack.

"Where's the real vanilla?" Saylor asked, shifting the Lazy Susan around. "This imitation stuff makes my sugar cookies taste like they came out of a package. And besides, do you know how they make this stuff?"

"I do," said Brig. "It's disgusting."

"How do they make imitation vanilla?" asked Scout.

"Google it," grinned Brig.

"Do not google that," said Saylor. "Trust me."

Having seen the process for herself on the Science Channel, Saylor threw the imitation bottle out. But she was still having trouble finding the real deal. She wanted this meal to be perfect. Everything needed to be perfect for tonight.

"Forget the vanilla," said Scout. "You said yes to Jeff's proposal."

"Actually, no."

Two pairs of blue eyes narrowed on her.

"What I mean is; *I* asked *him*. He said yes to me."

Now those blue gazes widened.

"And...Nick knows?" said Scout.

"Nick and I broke up."

There was an exchange of doubtful looks that passed between her sisters. Saylor usually got this treatment from Scout and the twins. Brig was the youngest. What was she doing exchanging looks with Scout? Brig hadn't even had her first boyfriend yet, just a series of crushes on her male teachers and soccer coaches.

"What happened?" asked Scout.

Saylor did not want to rehash what had happened earlier at Nick's apartment. It wouldn't be the first time she'd told her sisters about her suspicions of Nick's infidelities. By the next look her sisters exchanged, Saylor knew that they were guessing the truth.

As per her usual, Saylor opened her mouth to defend Nick. Only this time, nothing came out. There was nothing to say. She'd caught him cheating. Again.

Saylor leaned against the counter, waiting for the pain in her chest. Like her mouth, her heart was silent. There was nothing left to break. He'd hurt her callously. Again.

Only this time, he hadn't come after her. He

hadn't called to explain away what she'd seen. He hadn't texted to rewrite the history she'd witnessed.

"So, you and Jeff?" said Brig.

"It's not real." Saylor found her voice and straightened. When she turned, her gaze met her youngest sister. "Oh Brig, were you interested in him?"

The thought of that made Saylor's heart hurt. The pain wasn't at the thought of hurting her sister. The pain was at the thought of releasing Jeff to her sister.

"Not at all." Brig emphasized each word through her huge grin. "I think you two make the perfect couple."

"It's not real," Saylor repeated. She felt a cool balm of relief now that she knew she wouldn't have to hand Jeff over.

Saylor turned her attention back to the search for the real vanilla. She finally found it in the back of the cabinets. There was just enough in the small glass vial for one batch of cookies.

"We're just doing this so that we can save the ranch," said Saylor. "I'm done with men."

Saylor didn't need to turn around to know that her sisters were sharing another look. Instead, she scooped the dough out of the bowl and began spreading it on the baking sheet, concentrating on making perfect circles. A hand came on her shoulder.

"I think you made the right decision," said Scout. "Jeff is a good man. He's going to be good to you."

The words weren't an imitation. They were real. Saylor could feel the truth of them seeping into the cracks of her heart. Just as she had felt the warmth of Jeff when she'd rested her head against his chest the other night.

Ever since they'd pulled away from the apartment, Saylor had felt as though something was shifting inside her. She and Jeff hadn't talked much on the car ride. If that had been Nick, she'd have tried hard to fill the silence. But sitting with Jeff, she hadn't felt the need to say or do anything.

Saylor had just had one of the most embarrassing things in her life happen. Jeff had witnessed it all. Instead of dragging her over it and telling her what he thought she should do, he'd exposed his secret pain.

At the thought of Jeff in pain, Saylor felt pinpricks in her heart. Not the stabbing wounds she felt every time Nick disappointed her. Or any of the times he implied she was lacking in some area, which was why he had to go outside of their relationship to have his needs met.

The back door opened. And there he was. Not Nick. He wouldn't come to the ranch unless he was dragged, which would happen if any of her sisters got a hand on him. It was Jeff who stood in the backdoor alongside Jackson.

"Hey," said Jeff, his gaze finding and holding hers.

"Hi," said Saylor.

"I was just coming to check on you."

The warmth wasn't seeping through the cracks of her heart any longer. It spread uniformly through her as if her heart had never been broken in the first place.

Had Nick ever come to check on her? Had he ever come after her? She had always been the one to seek out and chase after him.

"Nice work, bro," said Brig.

"They know?" asked Jeff, coming to stand beside her.

Saylor was so focused on the feeling in her heart that her mouth refused to work. So, she simply nodded.

"How are you holding up?" asked Jeff.

Wait? Wasn't that her job? To check on him? To ask after him?

"Come walk with me." Jeff held out his right arm. His left was caught up in the sling.

Saylor took Jeff's arm. She wrapped her left arm around his. And then, for good measure, she rested her right hand in the crook of his elbow.

The sun was lower in the sky. A cool breeze blew as they walked away from the house. Saylor was so warm where her body contacted Jeff's that she shivered at the contrast.

Jeff dropped his hold on her. Saylor wanted to protest. A moment later, he shrugged out of his coat. It looked to be a chore with only one arm operable.

Saylor reached to help him rid himself of the jacket. But by then, he was already done. And then she was being encased in his warmth.

Not just his heat, but his scent. Spice and earth and Jeff. Saylor was at a loss for words. Mainly because every time she breathed in, she got a strong whiff of him. She closed her eyes and soaked him in. When she opened her eyes, she saw him looking at her.

"I told them it wasn't real," Saylor rushed to assure him. "That this was all fake. I won't be a bother."

She wanted to chide herself for being caught in such a silly fantasy. Nick would've never stood for such a reaction as sniffing his coat. Wait? Had Nick ever given Saylor his coat when he thought she was cold?

"You do realize I'm getting the best part of this deal," said Jeff, looping up her arm to rest inside the crook of his. "A beautiful wife on my arm. Who is one of the kindest, most capable women I've ever met."

"I..." Saylor didn't know how to complete that sentence. "You don't have to say things like that."

"What? The truth? Has no one ever told you that you are beautiful, Saylor?"

"Well, my mom. But she's supposed to say things like that."

"Saylor, you're breathtaking."

She shook her head. "You've never seen my sister, Mareen. We could've been twins, even though we have different mothers. But she got all the best features."

"I've never met Mareen. I've only met you, and I stand by what I said. I never lie."

Saylor wanted to believe that. She'd made excuse after excuse for Nick, who never proved her right. Not even once.

Jeff had never once proven her wrong. Maybe she should believe him?

"Come." Jeff tugged her toward the cabin. "I think you should rest. I don't like those bags under your eyes."

Jeff's hand moved to the small of her back. But the warmth was gone in light of that last comment.

I don't like those bags under your eyes.

Saylor had known it was too good to be true. He'd already found something wrong with her. Less than a day into this new relationship and she already wasn't good enough.

CHAPTER SIXTEEN

They weren't married yet. Still, Jeff wished he could lift Saylor in his arms and carry her over the threshold of the cabin. He'd have to settle for holding her hand as he led her through the front door.

Jeff had only been in the cabin a week. But from the first day he'd set his foot in here, it had felt like home. Now he knew it had everything to do with the woman beside him whose hands had helped build this place.

He wanted to start his life with her here. Maybe they could add on to the structure in the coming years. This time they would build it together.

At the thought of the work, Jeff felt another tingle of sensation in his left arm. He wanted to get an appointment with the VA clinic soon. Perhaps this increased neurological activity spelled something good for him?

He'd long since given up hope that he'd ever had the complete use of his left arm again. With Saylor now in his life, he was experiencing more and more sensations on a daily basis. Maybe it was his arm that had different ideas about its prognosis now that the woman of his dreams was within reach.

"I was making you my famous sugar cookies," Saylor said as Jeff shut the door behind them. "They're always a big hit at gatherings."

"I can't wait to try them later. Right now, you need to rest."

"I still have chores to tend to," Saylor protested as he led her into the bedroom. "And I need to check on horses."

"I'll take care of that," he said.

Jeff got the impression that Saylor was always on call, especially with that ex who couldn't seem to do anything for himself. Those times were over. He was going to look after her, starting with her health and well-being. Then he'd move on to see if she could let him into her heart.

For now, he turned her around to face him.

Saylor looked flustered. But she wasn't fighting him, which let him see just how tired she was.

"If there's an emergency or something I can't handle in the next couple of hours, I'll come wake you. But for now, I want you to get some rest."

Saylor lowered her head so that all he saw of her was the top of the hairband that gathered her brown locks into a ponytail. Jeff itched to wrestle the tie away so that her hair would fall around her shoulders. But that was not his place. Not yet.

"I have eye make up," she said.

He frowned. He must have been so caught up thinking about her hair that he'd missed part of the conversation.

"To cover the bags under my eyes." Saylor waved in the vicinity of her eyes even though her head was still down.

With his index finger, Jeff lifted Saylor's chin until she met his gaze. "I don't want you to hide anything anymore."

By the time he was done showing this woman all the care in his heart, she wouldn't have a single load to carry. Not under her eyes. Not on her back. And certainly, not in her heart.

"We're partners now," he continued. "We're going to share our load."

Saylor's brows pulled together. The move made the dark circles under her beautiful blues look as though they were bruised. Jeff couldn't stand it any longer.

"Lie back," he said, and she did. "I'll take care of it."

As Saylor slipped out of her shoes and gathered her legs onto the mattress, Jeff pulled the sheets up to her chin. Then, because he couldn't help himself, he pressed a kiss to her forehead. It was just a light press, a whisper of the affection he truly wanted to give to her.

Though it was a whisper, he let the soft caress linger. He wasn't sure how long he held there. When he pulled away, Saylor's eyes were already closed.

Jeff pressed a kiss to each of her eyelids in turn. "I'll take care of everything."

He stayed and stared at her for long moments. She was his. They only had the words between them. Soon it would be legal. She could call it fake all she wanted, but he was going to prove to her that his feelings were real.

Jeff had accomplished his mission. He'd gotten Saylor away from Nick.

No, actually, he hadn't. Saylor had done that

herself. Which was why this time, the break up would last.

"You did it," Brig said when he shut the front door of the cabin. "How did you do it? Is Nick still alive? Because if he's not, I won't mind."

"I didn't do anything," said Jeff. "Saylor decided."

Brig's frown was doubtful. As though she suspected Jeff was holding out on her.

"Really, she did it all herself. I was simply there to pick up the pieces."

"She doesn't know, does she?" asked Brig.

"Know what?" said Jeff.

"That you're in love with her."

Jeff didn't correct the youngest Silver sister. He was in love with Saylor. Had been since the first moment he'd seen her from a distance. Had known it to be true the first time he saw her with a horse and saw the gentle spirit who wanted to heal wounds. Now he was going to be her protector. He was going to help her heal from the years of emotional and mental abuse she'd suffered.

"Just marry her quick," said Brig as they walked along. "I'm sure Nick will come sniffing around here soon. Likely when his clean laundry runs out."

"She's not going back this time." Jeff was sure of it.

Out in the pastures, they saw Bingley ambling along. The horse wasn't running or eating with the other horses, but he was upright.

Saylor had said the colicky horse might not want to eat for a few days while his stomach calmed down. It was clear that whatever parasites that had invaded Bingley's body were making their way out.

The horse was in much better spirits this morning. He made his way over to Jeff. Bingley placed his muzzle over the fence in a clear sign that he wanted a pat.

Jeff obliged the animal. He looked into the blond horse's deep, soulful eyes. Just the other day, the horse had writhed in agony, searching for relief. Now, with the attention and care he was receiving, Bingley was on the mend.

"It's all gonna be fine, buddy," Jeff soothed. "You just gotta be patient while it works its way out of your system."

That's exactly what he'd be while Saylor worked The Ex out of her system. Jeff was going to hold her, feed her, pet her, and anything else Saylor allowed him to do until she was a brand-new woman. His brand-new woman.

CHAPTER SEVENTEEN

For the second night in a row, Saylor woke easily from sleep. Her toes were toasty under the covers, not exposed to the cold night air. Her body was cradled in the soft, pillow-top mattress, not the firm brick that Nick had at his apartment. But she knew she was not in her own bed. She smelled the heady musk of man on the pillowcase.

With that thought, Saylor bolted upright. She was in a man's bed. Laying under sheets that smelled like him. Awareness brightened all around her as the sun set out the window.

She'd slept the day away. In Jeff's bed.

Instead of feeling panicked, Saylor felt a sense of calm wash over her. Instead of feeling shame at being in another man's bed, she felt a sense of rightness. Jeff wasn't some other man. He was her fiancé. He'd only known her for a week, and he'd agreed to marry her.

Very soon, waking up in his bed could be her life. Climbing into the bed with Jeff tucking her in. Falling asleep against Jeff's chest. Waking up with Jeff's scent all around her. The only thing that was missing was him.

The sun was low in the sky outside the window. It looked more like the evening was approaching than a new morning. Looking over at the clock on the table beside the bed, she saw that it was only early evening.

She hadn't slept the day away. She'd only taken a nap. Just that slight bit of rest had made her feel renewed.

A beep sounded from the table beside the bed. There was a phone lying there. Unlike her phone that was wrapped in a pastel covering, this phone was black with no case. It had to be Jeff's phone.

There had been many times when Nick would leave his phone out. Saylor had gotten in the habit of looking away from the messages that would pop up. She'd learned her lesson when a casual glance would shatter her heart at the sight of an inappropriate emoji sent to a man who had a girlfriend.

So, Saylor had gotten in the habit of only reaching out to turn the phone over so that she didn't see the women texting her boyfriend, making demands on his time, his attention, his body. Demands that Nick was always more than happy to fill. Demands he'd cater to when he could never keep his promises to her. Not even the basic, unwritten one of fidelity.

Saylor wasn't with Nick any longer. She was now with Jeff. A man who listened when she talked. A man who sought her out for her company. A man who offered her his hand not only in her work on the ranch but because he was a gentleman and insisted on treating her like a lady.

Jeff's phone beeped again. Saylor glanced over. And then wished she hadn't.

A message popped up on the rectangular face of the cellphone. Saylor was just far enough away that the letters were unclear. She had no need to look closely.

Jeff wasn't Nick. This relationship would be different. In fact, she should find Jeff and give him his phone. Which would mean getting nearer to the device and risk making sense of the words there.

The door to the bedroom opened. Saylor snatched her hand back. Jeff filled the doorway. His smile was the brightest thing she'd seen this day.

"You're awake," he said, coming to the edge of the bed. "How do you feel?"

"Fine." Saylor took a deep breath. Clucking that word off her tongue, she tried again. "I mean, good. I'm good."

"That rest did you good. Your eyes are shining bright again."

Jeff tilted his head as he gazed down at her. There was no judgment in his gaze. No, that looked like satisfaction and a touch of delight in his light brown eyes.

The phone on the bedside table chirped again. Both of their gazes went to it. Now that she was sitting up, Saylor could see the letters stringing together. They formed words in her mind.

Call me back. I need you.

Saylor blinked, but the words wouldn't go away. She tried to pull up the list of what that could mean, like all the times she'd done when she'd seen similar messages on Nick's phone. But none of the excuses of the past were within her mental reach.

Jeff reached for the phone. He sat down on the edge of the bed as he swiped up to unlock the device. He didn't slip the phone into his pocket. He held it in the palm of his hands where she could clearly see the message.

Instead of looking at the message, Saylor chose to look at his face. Jeff didn't seem pleased at the message. He appeared weary.

Saylor wanted to reach out to him. She wanted to offer him comfort for whatever hurt this woman was bringing into his world. And yes, it was a woman's name at the top of the message.

"It's my mom," said Jeff.

It took Saylor's fogged brain long moments to understand the meaning of his words. It was his mother asking him to call her back. It was his mother telling her son that she needed him.

"She only ever calls when my dad needs something."

Right. His dad. The one who abused his mom.

Jeff let out a weary sigh as he placed the phone back on the bedside table. Saylor reached for his arm, only to find that she held the left arm, which was in the sling.

Jeff looked down at her hand. Saylor made a move to yank her hands from him, but he covered her hand with his right one, ensuring her hold on him.

"People always ask; why doesn't she leave."

Jeff didn't meet her gaze. He kept his eyes on her hand. His thumb rubbed over her knuckles as she ran her own thumb in a circular motion on his forearm. She knew he couldn't feel it, but she had a suspicion that watching the motion soothed him nonetheless.

"No one ever asks what's wrong with him. They always blame the victim."

Jeff lifted his head to her then. His gaze penetrated hers, letting her see a vulnerable side she'd never been privy to with any male on less than four feet.

"The physical violence stopped about a year ago when he became sick. But the mental violence, the emotional violence continues. I think it's worse now that he can't raise his fist. I know she needs help, but whenever I reach out, I get pulled into that hurt as well."

Saylor pulled him to her. She worried she'd overstepped after a second when he didn't hold her back. His left arm rested between them. But he didn't place his right hand around her.

Instead, he buried his nose in her neck. The deep inhale he took sent a shiver down her spine.

The exhale a moment later brought her closer to him than she'd ever been to anyone in her life.

They stayed like that for long moments. Possibly an hour. When he finally pulled away, the sun had set.

"Come on," he said. "Let's go get you fed."

CHAPTER EIGHTEEN

The bounty of food before him was a feast for the eyes and nose. A roast ham covered in pineapple slices pinned with cloves promised dessert as the main course. Collard greens marinated in the leftover pieces of the hog, like the ham's hock, guaranteed that the sweet tooth would be satisfied.

Jeff's fork remained where it had been placed next to his plate over twenty minutes ago. Not a morsel of the dishes touched his mouth. It was very likely that he was going to starve, and he had no qualms about it.

There was a grumbling of need in his gut. It wasn't his stomach. Jeff's hunger was for the woman at his side.

His right arm was wrapped around the top of Saylor's chair. Every time she leaned back to put her fork in her mouth, her nape brushed the fleshy part at the back of his thumb and set off fireworks at his fingertips. Her soft hair tickled his palm, urging him to capture the strands in his fingers. With his right hand so occupied with being close to Saylor, it had no interest in going near his own cutlery.

Jeff's left arm was in his sling. Though it was captured and held, he swore he felt twinges of sensation every now and again. The twinges happened each and every time Saylor's skin brushed against his. It was as though he wanted to reach out and pull her to him with that arm that hadn't felt much since the blast destroyed his nerve endings.

"You're not hungry?" Saylor asked, her fork paused at her mouth.

Jeff had to take a deep breath before he could tear his gaze away from those lush lips. Oh, how he envied that fork.

"I can get you something else if you don't like it."

Jeff was still staring at her lips, which was why he caught the slight tremble there. Saylor bit her lip as though she were uncertain. Her gaze cast downward at his untouched plate.

With the greatest of reluctance, Jeff slipped his arm from around her shoulders. He picked up his fork and shoveled a heaping helping in his mouth. He'd made the move to stave off her worry that he didn't like her cooking. The moment the food hit his tongue, Jeff's eyes went to his hairline. He couldn't help his grin of pure bliss as he swallowed the bite.

That grin spread even wider when he saw Saylor watching him. Her lips still trembled. Though this time, they shook with a small laugh of delight.

Jeff watched Saylor move through opposing expressions. If just the simple act of showing his enjoyment of a meal she helped prepare for him made her happy, then he'd have this woman on Cloud Nine for the rest of her days now that he'd be by her side.

Something flared in Saylor's blue gaze. The delight shifted into something that looked like sparks of interest, of want, of desire. Jeff had every intention of fanning those flames into something as close to love as he could get them. Because that was what was in his heart.

Saylor was so easy to love. Her every thought was to be of aid to others. Her every move was to be a comforting light. That light had been smothered for years.

No longer. Jeff was prepared to turn himself into kindling if that's what she needed to stay bright. He would shine his light of love so fiercely upon this woman until she knew what it meant to be cherished.

"When's the big day for you two?"

Saylor blinked at the sound of Linc's voice. It took her another second to tear her gaze away from Jeff's. Jeff allowed his eyes to linger on her beautiful profile.

"We have a couple of months," said Saylor.

"Why wait?" said Jeff.

Saylor blinked again when her gaze connected once more with his. Her lashes fluttered over her baby blues like she was a bird feeling the warmth of the sun on its face for the first time.

"A-are you sure?" she stammered.

"About spending the rest of my life with you?"

The blush that pinkened her cheeks was endearing. Jeff couldn't wait until he had the right to lay featherlight kisses on those cheeks.

"Yes, Saylor, I'm sure."

Saylor brushed a stray hair from her temple. That strand had escaped the ponytail she'd gathered her tresses back into. Unlike her normal style, this queue was loose, allowing many of her strands to rest around her face. Jeff couldn't wait until he had the right to rip the band off and let her hair flow free every day.

"I vote for sooner," Brig piped in. "Everything from Scout's wedding is still here, including the flowers."

"Well," said Tilly, "looks like you'll be able to schedule it soon. Here comes the man who could make it happen."

All eyes around the dinner table went to the back door where Father Matthews was striding up to the porch. No one rose to open the door for him. This hadn't been the first time their next-door neighbor had stopped in at the ranch. Aside from being General Silver's lifelong best friend, Father Matthews was like a second father to the Silver sisters, and this house was like a second home for him.

"Evening, hellions," Father Matthews said with a jovial grin on his face.

"Evening, Father," the four girls all said in their faux angelic voices.

"Pull up a chair," said Scout rising from her place. "I'll fix you a plate."

"This is actually more than a social call," said Father Matthews. "I came to see Saylor."

"Is something wrong with one of your horses?" said Saylor, her body already tensing to rise and jump into action.

"No." Father Matthews shook his head. His head tilted as he looked at Jeff's arm strewn across the back of the chair. His brow raised when he met Jeff's gaze. "The horses are fine. I was in town, and I ran into Nick Murphy."

A cold wind breezed through the dining room at the name of The Ex-Boyfriend. It was as though the holy man had spoken a curse.

Under Jeff's arm, Saylor stiffened. He cupped her shoulder cap, trying to let her know he was here. If he was being honest with himself, he'd admit that the move was more of a staking claim. Saylor was his. Nothing The Ex-Boyfriend could say or do would change that.

Father Matthews' gaze narrowed, as though he could hear Jeff's thoughts. There was a slight upturn to his mustached mouth. Jeff couldn't tell if it was amusement or disapproval. For all Father Matthews knew, Jeff was the interloper in Saylor's relationship.

It didn't matter. Jeff would've wanted the man's approval. But he was moving forward with this marriage regardless of what Father Matthews thought of him.

"Nick was asking about your father's will and the marriage clause," said Father Matthews. "When I asked why he wanted to know, he said it was because he was thinking about marrying you."

The slight intake of breath that gushed from Saylor's lips was enough to knock Jeff down. He knew he wasn't mistaken that he'd heard the tiniest sliver of hope in that inhale. Jeff had to stop his nails from digging into Saylor's shoulder to hold her in place.

Saylor sat forward. She didn't rise. However, it was just far enough forward that she was no longer within Jeff's reach as his right arm now hung limp on the back of the chair.

CHAPTER NINETEEN

Because he was thinking about marrying you.

Father Matthews' words kept swirling around in Saylor's head. What had Nick been thinking seeking out the pastor? Why hadn't he called her himself? Would she have even answered the phone if he had? Where was her phone?

Those thoughts were soon drowned by the conversation all around Saylor. The voices in the kitchen sounded like the hum of a Charlie Brown cartoon. Fog moved into her brain. Her temples were pounding, begging for the press of her thumbs to ease the ache. Her ears demanded her palms cover them, so they stopped the ringing she heard.

"You caught him with another woman."

"You're not going back to him this time."

"He is the worst man in the world. You deserve better."

Her sisters all spoke at once, so Saylor didn't know who said what. The cacophony of sounds harmonized into a needle scratching on vinyl. With a repeated chorus of nails screeching down the world's longest chalkboard.

A brush of warmth cleared all thoughts and sounds away. Like the sun drying up an errant puddle on the floor, Jeff's fingertips brushed against the exposed skin of her shoulder. At his touch, all Saylor could think about was turning her head into his chest and resting.

Her sisters' voices made her feel heavy with shame and self-doubt. Her thoughts of Nick made her feel weary and tired. The feel of Jeff? That refreshed her, drowning the others out with his calming reassurance.

Jeff said nothing to her. He only looked her over. His gaze skated over the tension of her tight shoulders. They took in the indecision on her furrowed brow. They rested a moment on her quivering lips as they vacillated on her response.

"Would you all excuse us," Jeff said. His words were firm. Not a question.

With a scrape of wooden legs against the floor, he scooted his chair back and stood. Then he offered his hand to Saylor. She stared at it before placing her hand in his. When he tugged, she came willingly, as though this man would lead her toward salvation.

All around them, the room fell into a hushed silence. That was a neat trick. Not even their parents could ever get the Silver sisters to quiet down all at once.

Jeff's gaze was intent on hers as they left the dining room. Saylor wanted nothing more than to go back to the cabin and lay down inside the cradle of his strong chest. She wanted to rest her cheek against there and listen only to his heartbeat.

Jeff had never once made her feel that there was something wrong with her for staying with Nick. He'd never made any comments about her choices in partners that reflected badly on the woman she was. He'd only ever offered his compassion and understanding and his kindness.

This man was going to marry her. True, it was going to be a fake relationship. But Jeff would never lie to her, or question her decisions like her sisters, or make her feel like someone who would never be enough like Nick had done for the duration of their relationship.

"Are you gonna reach out to him?" Jeff asked as they began to climb the stairs.

It took Saylor a moment to answer. She was more focused on lifting her legs to conquer the stairs. She had expected that she and Jeff would leave the house and head back to the cabins. Instead, they were headed to the second floor of the house where the bedrooms were.

Saylor opened her mouth to say no in response to Jeff's question. The word wouldn't come out. There was some part of her that held back.

Nick had reached out to her. Well, not exactly out to her. But he had metaphorically lifted a finger. In the past, it was always Saylor who made the first move when he'd had an indiscretion. He'd take his time in responding, but he always responded. He always came back to her, just as true loves did.

Jeff's sigh was nearly soundless, but Saylor felt the slight slump in his tall frame. His gaze shuttered, but only for a second. He pursed his lips as though he wanted to keep words in. Unlike her, he let them out.

"He was with another woman." Jeff's words were terse. "You know that. You saw it."

Technically, she hadn't seen it. Just the evidence that pointed to it. But she hadn't actually seen Holly inside that apartment.

"You deserve better."

Saylor tried not to flinch as he threw her sister's words back at her. There was that implication again that she was settling when she had done her best in this relationship. She had fought for what she wanted. Though all the fight was gone out of her now.

Saylor was tired. All she wanted was to be held. But Jeff was barely touching her. And then he was.

Jeff pressed his lips to her forehead. It was a chaste kiss, confirming what she already knew. He was only doing this, offering to marry her, out of a sense of duty. It would never be love.

Still, her heart raced. It ached to have him feel something in return. Her heart ached for him to yearn for her as she was doing for him.

"Which one is yours?" Jeff asked as he pulled away from her.

Saylor pointed wordlessly to her bedroom door. Even though her finger wanted to riot and point back down the stairs and across the way to the cabin where he would be sleeping.

They walked the few steps to her door together,

side by side. Jeff wasn't touching her, and she wanted him to. She just wasn't sure how to ask for it.

She opened her mouth. But once again, no words came out. Saylor choked as indecision obstructed her throat.

Jeff stepped back at her silence. Before she'd even turned the knob, he'd already disappeared down the steps. Saylor closed her door behind her and sank down on her bed.

She had already slept a few hours, but she felt as though she hadn't slept in weeks. Her head aimed for her pillow, but before it made it there, she saw her phone charging on her nightstand.

Glancing at it, she saw that there were ten missed calls from Nick. Beneath the calls flashed an alert for unread text messages. Swiping her thumb over her phone, she read the missives.

Give me another chance.

I need you.

CHAPTER TWENTY

That had been the wrong thing to say. But it had been the truth. Saylor did deserve better.

Jeff had known better than to push her. All the years of watching his mother endure the violence of his father, he'd read enough pamphlets from women's shelters, watched enough online intervention videos, and spoken to enough school counselors and social workers to know.

He knew the script that he was supposed to follow. He knew he was supposed to make Saylor feel heard, not judged. He knew his words should aim to validate her feelings, not blame or shame her for how she had reacted in the past. Because, in truth, Saylor had done nothing wrong.

She had trusted someone who was a liar. She had loved someone who was unworthy. She had stayed with someone who was disloyal.

None of that was her fault.

Jeff had slipped up with his last words to her. Because his words were also true. Saylor did deserve better.

Jeff wanted to punch a wall. Not with his right hand. He felt the tingles in his left palm, which was cradled in a sling. Instead of being joyful at the sensations there, he wanted to use that energy to commit violence.

Walking out of the front door, Jeff stopped as he came to the fencing that separated the front yard from the first pasture. He inhaled deeply, trying to calm the ire inside him. It took all the fresh air of the night to get his wayward emotions under control.

He hadn't felt this out of control since he was a teenager wanting to throw his fists at any and everyone who dared cross him. He'd grown up helpless to stop the violence against his mother. Helpless to get her to see the wrongness of it.

Jeff had joined the military because he'd had rage in him. His commanders always pointed him in the direction of the true bad guys, the ones who committed heinous acts against the innocent. Jeff had never felt an iota of remorse when he took down an insurgent.

And wasn't that what Nick was, an insurgent? The villain committed heinous acts against Saylor. Acts that had crumbled her infrastructure and weakened her spirit.

Saylor didn't have a physical mark on her from Nick's attention. It was his lack of attention that had left the woman bruised and blackened. And for that, Jeff wanted to wring the man's neck.

Just like that, all of the control he'd fought for with those deep breaths left him on an exhale. Jeff unwrapped his left arm from the sling. Instead of the arm remaining cocked or his fingers clenching into a fist, the arm slumped to his side.

"You look ready for a fight."

Jeff didn't turn to see Wilson come up behind him. He knew one of his brothers would be tracking his movements and keeping watch. Not that any of them suspected the anger he was now trying to keep under wraps. He'd always been cool while in combat.

"Did she call the wedding off?" asked Wilson.

"No, she didn't," said Jeff.

"But your trigger finger is still itching for a fight."

Wilson was looking at the prone fingers of his left hand.

"She might call it off," Jeff admitted. "She might go back to him."

Wilson whistled low. "Then she's not the girl for you. If she does go back to him, then she'll only get what she deserves."

Jeff wheeled on his friend. "You think she deserves to be treated like that? To be cheated on? To be someone's doormat?"

"If that's what she wants."

Jeff was close to punching out one of his closest friends. He might have if Wilson's chin was high and tilted to the left. Just the perfect angle for Jeff to connect with a right hook.

They all had long suspected that Wilson had a death wish. He blamed himself for the General's death. After all, the General had shoved Wilson out of the way just before the bomb went off. Had Wilson still been standing in that space, it would've been his funeral months ago, and the general would be here with his daughters.

When Jeff's fists failed to connect to Wilson's chin, the man lowered his head and went on.

"She's not a stupid woman. None of these Silver women are. They had the General for a father. She can get out if she wants. Maybe she doesn't want to."

Jeff tried to swallow, but he couldn't get that lump down his throat. His mother could've left his father. Years ago, Jeff had provided her with the financial means to do so. But she'd funneled the money to pay off his father's debts. Meanwhile, they continued to live in squalor. Because she didn't want to leave. Because she claimed she loved him. That he was her world.

For all of his life, Jeff had never understood that sentiment. Now he did. In just a week, Saylor had captured his heart, his body, his soul.

He didn't want to leave.

Because he loved her.

She had become his world.

Jeff needed to go back into the house. He needed to go back up the stairs. He needed to go back to the script.

Tell Saylor that he was sorry for what had happened to her.

That she wasn't to blame for what Nick had done to her.

That he couldn't pass judgment on her decisions of the past.

That she'd had her reasons for staying.

True, Jeff believed all those reasons were false. Saylor didn't believe she was beautiful. She believed men needed a long leash. But neither of those were true.

Saylor was beautiful and desirable. All men did not cheat. Just the ones who were too weak to stand next to a good woman.

Jeff was that man. He would stand next to Saylor. He would tell her she took his breath away every day. She would see his desire for her in his every look, in his every touch. He would never even think of straying.

He looked down at his phone. The message his mother had sent him earlier was still on the face of his phone, left unanswered. His mother had made a choice. She knew her options, but she wanted to stay with her husband.

Saylor had never believed she had a choice. He'd just given her one upstairs. Now he just needed her to choose him.

Before he could take a step back toward the house, he heard footsteps coming down the front porch. In the moonlight, Jeff saw a woman's figure rushing to the parked cars. All of the Silver sisters favored one another. But he could tell Saylor's frame from a mile away.

Jeff wasn't a mile away. Saylor was climbing into a car. Jeff's heart sank that he knew where she was headed to at this time of night. It looked like she had made her choice, and she was headed back to The Boyfriend.

CHAPTER TWENTY-ONE

Saylor paralleled parked in front of the building. It was rare at this time of night that there was a space available, especially one right in front of Nick's apartment building.

She looked down at her phone before she reached to unbuckle her belt. Her mind went to Jeff as she clicked the red button. She sat forward a little, feeling the strap's hold on her.

The seatbelt was there to protect her from harm. It offered a sense of security in the world that whizzed by her. Much like being held in Jeff's caress. Though the seatbelt wasn't as warm as Jeff. Still, the belt let her go after she clicked the release. Much like Jeff had let her go once he'd delivered her safely to her bedroom.

Saylor had expected him to argue with her. She'd expected Jeff to rail against Nick like her sisters had done at dinner. She'd expected him to fight with her over her decisions to remain in her relationship with Nick. She'd hoped Jeff would fight for her. Instead, he'd walked away from her.

You deserve better.

Did she? She certainly hoped so. She stepped out of the car, prepared to get the better she was due.

Looking down at her phone, Saylor saw the unanswered text messages from Nick. Even his words were all about him, asking her to do things for him.

Give me another chance. Not even a please. *I need you.* What about her needs?

Nick had never given a care to her. He hadn't even come after her directly. He'd sent Father Matthews to fetch her. Well, that type of behavior was stopping right here and right now.

All these years, she'd given so much of herself to this man when he never gave her a single thing. Except for a set of his house keys.

Saylor had treasured having this single key added to her key chain. Though Nick had only given her the bottom lock. Not the top one. So that if he was home, she still needed his permission to enter.

Saylor didn't use the key as she came to Nick's door. She knocked. It took a moment for a response. As Nick came to the locked door, Saylor heard the rattling of locks. Not just of the bottom lock, but the top one as well. Clearly, Nick wasn't alone.

That was confirmed when the door was flung open. Nick stood there, shirtless. Hair mussed. A twenty-dollar bill in his hand.

"Saylor!"

The color drained from his face. He shifted from barefoot to barefoot. Beads of sweat appeared between his two perfectly manicured brows.

How many times had she seen this exact same scenario? Her supposed boyfriend, blocking a scene he didn't want her to see. His mouth working to weave a story that was too flimsy to be considered for a doily.

What was different this time was that instead of looking away, Saylor stared openly at the mussed pillows on the sofa and the discarded high heels on the rug. Instead of searching for comforting, compliant words, she lifted a brow of her own and watched him squirm.

"What are you doing here?" said Nick, angling

his body so that Saylor couldn't see any further into the apartment.

Before Saylor could respond with the rehearsed speech she'd made, a feminine voice beat her to it.

"She's back? Really?" Holly Marks came into view. She wore Nick's old football jersey and nothing else. "Girl, have you no self-respect?"

"I do, actually," said Saylor, pressing her hand to her chest. "Do you?"

Holly smirked at that, cocking a hip. "My boyfriend isn't community property."

"Well, he's not my boyfriend anymore. I broke up with him last night when he was with you. Which means the chain of custody passes to you."

All color leached from Holly's face. She straightened, shifting from foot to foot as Nick had done when he'd seen Saylor standing on the threshold.

"Look, Saylor," Nick said, using his soothing voice. "There's nothing going on between her and me. Just two old friends hanging out."

Holly's features contorted with disgust. She turned on her heel, grabbed a rumpled dress from the back of the couch, and headed for the bathroom.

"It's fine," said Saylor.

Nick's brows rose in suspicion. Then they lowered, all perspiration sliding away and drying up.

"It's my fault," Saylor continued. "I should've assumed you would have company. I just came to return your keys."

Saylor reached for Nick's hand. She dropped the solitary key in his palm. Then she turned and walked down the steps.

With each step away from him, Saylor felt a load lift from her shoulders. There was only a small part of her that protested. The part of her that believed that if you loved someone, you came back.

Nick had never come after her. Not once. She'd always chased after him. This would be the last time.

Before she got out the outer door of the apartment building, someone grabbed her arm. Saylor turned to find Nick behind her.

"Saylor, I told you, she doesn't mean anything to me."

"That's the problem." Saylor yanked her arm, but he didn't let go. "Women should mean something to you. I should've meant something. But no one means anything to you, except you."

"Saylor, we can work on this."

What he meant was that she could do all the

work. She didn't want that. She wanted someone to look after her as much as she looked after him. She wanted someone who made her feel strong, not tired. She didn't want someone who came back to her. She wanted someone who would never let her go in the first place.

She wanted Jeff.

"Let me go," she said to Nick.

Saylor yanked her arm again, but Nick wouldn't let go. Then with a high-pitched cry, he was flying through the air. When she looked up, Jeff stood between the two of them.

CHAPTER TWENTY-TWO

*J*eff had had no orders to engage The Ex. But the second he'd seen his hands-on Saylor, he'd lost it. Nick was lucky he'd been shoved away. Jeff's right fist was cocked, ready to do serious damage to the man's face. His left hand was itching to get into the fight. His boots ached to dance a tune on the man's chest. But something held him back.

Saylor.

She held onto his left arm. He shouldn't have felt it. But he did.

He felt the imprint of her thumb on his bicep. He felt the heat of her chest against the back of his forearm. He felt the tug of her plea louder than any words she might say.

"Jeff?"

All Jeff could see was red. Nick was the enemy, and Jeff had to take him down before he could do any more destruction to the woman he loved.

Only, Jeff didn't want Saylor to see him like this. Like his father, standing in a rage over his mother, who was cowering on the floor. Begging, pleading. Insisting that she loved him even while she took his abuse as her due.

"Jeff?"

The sound of Saylor's voice broke him. Slowly, the red haze began to clear as Jeff came back to the present.

Nick was down on the ground. The pitiful excuse for a man crabbed walked backward, trying to put distance between himself and Jeff. His face was a dark mask of fear.

And wasn't that the irony. Having let go of his temper, Jeff had turned into the villain. He could never face Saylor again now that she knew that this was in him. Which was why he resisted when she tried to turn his face to meet hers.

"Jeff, look at me."

He couldn't. It was going to kill him to hear her take up for Nick. It was going to stop his heart to watch her go back into his arms.

Why wasn't she back in Nick's arms? Nick had managed to scramble to his feet. He was tripping up the steps of the apartment building. His arms were flung out, as though trying to protect himself from blows that weren't coming his way.

He wasn't even reaching out for Saylor. He wasn't even waiting for her. He was running away and leaving her behind.

The red haze threatened to come back to Jeff's eyes. Until bright blue blinded him.

"Are you okay?"

Jeff heard Saylor's words, but he had trouble deciphering them. She wasn't looking at Nick's retreating form. She wasn't looking into Jeff's confused gaze. Saylor held onto his right arm. She was checking on his hand, his fingers. Then she switched to his left hand.

"Did you hurt anything? Can you move your fingers?"

Still stunned, Jeff did as the veterinarian told him to. He was just a beast, after all. After years of training and careful control over his base instincts, he'd become what he feared. He'd become his father.

"Nothing's broken," Saylor said. Cradling his

bruised knuckles to her chest, she finally looked up into his eyes. "You came for me."

"Of course, I came for you."

With her free hand, Saylor brushed her fingers across his cheek. With the soft caress, something broke inside of Jeff. He turned his face into her hand and let out a shaky sigh.

Jeff inhaled the sweet scent of her. He had no idea how she was still here, in his arms? He fought to keep his hold loose. It was another battle he lost this night.

Once again, his right fist clenched. But this time, it wasn't to commit violence. It was an act of love. He wouldn't be able to hide it any longer. Nor would he be able to follow the script to help an abuse victim find the inner courage to leave her abuser.

"You thought I was going back to him," she said. "Didn't you?"

In response, Jeff pulled her closer. She didn't resist. She came to him willingly, resting both her hands against his chest. His heart leaped in response.

"I came to give him his keys. I was on my way back to you."

Jeff had to close his eyes again. The brightness of the light blue eyes gazing into his was overwhelming. Saylor hid nothing from him now. Not her vulnerability, nor her strength. She was both at the same time. And she trusted him to see it shining through.

"I want to marry you. Not because of the will and the ranch. I want to marry you because I want to be your wife. I want to take care of you and have you take care of me. I want to be your swan."

Jeff didn't need to hear anymore. He stopped her with a kiss. Not needing to open his eyes, his mouth found hers. He was a heat-seeking missile. He zeroed in on his target, and all around him, the world exploded.

He was blasted apart. Then flung back together. When his soul reknit itself, he felt an extra weight added to it. He felt a part of Saylor now living inside of him.

"I love you," he said when the fires inside him were cool enough to allow him to form words. "I felt something for you the first time you touched me."

"I want to say those words back to you," she said. "But I won't yet. For years, my definition of love was wrong. When I do tell you that I love you, I want you to know by my actions that I mean it."

Jeff pressed his lips to hers again. "I'll wait. I'll wait forever for you."

"I don't want you to wait. I want you always by my side."

"I will never leave it."

And with that, he twined their fingers together. Saylor rested her head in the crook of his neck. Jeff leaned his cheek on her forehead. To those walking by on the street, the two of them looked as though they were two swans entwined in a kiss.

"Wilson, you're not coming in for lunch?" asked Scout from the back porch of the big house.

Wilson shook his head in answer, his gaze on the horizon instead of the woman offering him an invitation. The sky was the same blue as Scout's eyes. Which were the same blue as her father's had been.

A blue so clear Wilson could see his own reflection and everything he'd done wrong that fateful day with General Abraham Silver. That clear blue was the last thing Wilson had seen right before the general lost his life.

Even from the distance Wilson had been from the man, Wilson had seen directly into the general's eyes. In that typically stern blue gaze, Wilson had seen a flash of fear, then resignation, then ... something Wilson hadn't been sure of. But the look was always near the forefront of Wilson's mind.

The shame at his failure to act was the only thing Wilson saw in his reflection these days. So he avoided mirrors, water, reflective surfaces, and every Silver girl whose eyes were just like her father's. Because Wilson knew he should've been the one who'd lost his life that day, not the old man. General Silver was far more valuable a man than Wilson Michaels could ever hope to be.

But here Wilson was, alive and well. Standing in the man's kitchen while his daughter filled his plate with food. Wilson sat the plate on the counter and turned to the back door.

"Where are you going?" called Scout.

"I've still got work to do," Wilson said to the floor.

Whatever words she said afterward were swallowed up by the screen door slamming behind him. Wilson quick-marched it away from the main house. He bypassed the stables, the barn, and the trails. He walked directly into the woods on an untrod path.

He kept his head low, unwilling to even look at the blue of the sky. He'd taken to getting up at night as the night's sky was dark and didn't remind him of that clear blue day when a blue-eyed man sacrificed his life for someone so unworthy.

Wilson should not be here. He did not why he was here. All he wanted to do was get lost and be alone.

Unfortunately, it sounded like he wouldn't get his wish today. A feminine yelp reached his eardrums. There was a woman out here and she was in danger.

Wilson picked up his pace in the once peaceful wooded area. He'd been one of the best trackers in his unit. So it took him no time at all to zero in on the location of the sound.

It came from a treehouse that looked like it had seen better days. The cracking and splintering of wood let him know someone was up there. Before he could think of how to climb up and get the woman down safely, a splintering sound boomed through the air.

The sound sent him back to that fateful day when the bomb had exploded. Wilson had seen blue eyes, then red flames, and finally black smoke.

When he looked up now, he saw a flash of ice, like a large snowflake. Or maybe a diamond. Was that a ring? It clunked to the ground at his feet.

Before he could reach down and investigate there was something red falling.

A woman in a red dress. Her limbs flailing as gravity turned on her. Wilson didn't hesitate. He scrambled into place to catch her before she hit the ground. She landed safely, and securely in his arms.

Her hair was a deep chestnut brown with honey highlights. Her nose was high and pert as though it was often tilted up towards the sun. Her lips were shaped like a bowstring; a perfect sideways heart that he felt the urge to tug at with his fingers to see if they would give.

Wilson's entire body warmed and came to life with this creature in his arms. It was the shock of awareness that nearly knocked him off his feet, not her weight. She was well built. Long legs, strong arms, and womanly curves. But her weight was slight. He could hold her for days. He wanted to hold her for days.

The warmth and the desire rattled him. It had been so long since he'd felt anything. Since he'd desired anyone.

More pieces of wood rained down on them. Wilson looked up. The treehouse was about twenty feet off the ground. If he hadn't been there to catch her, she definitely would've injured herself. Maybe even fatally.

A small cry left her lips as though she could sense her potential fate. He felt her cry like an arrow to his heart.

"It's all right," he said. "I've got you."

Slowly, her eyelids opened. The shock of blue behind her lids was a punch to Wilson's gut. He swore he saw the general peaking out from that blue reflection. His hands nearly dropped her then.

She was a Silver. She had to be. If not for that special brand of blue eyes, then just the fact that she was out here on the land.

Wilson had no desire to entangle himself in the fool plan of the general's daughters to get married to save the ranch. He of all men didn't deserve such happiness when he was at fault for the general's death.

He should be setting the general's daughter on her feet.

Instead, he cradled her to him as he looked into those reflective blue eyes.

"You saved me," she said.

"I did," was his reply.

He had.

Maybe this is why he was here?

Maybe the general had saved him so that he could save his daughter?

If so, then Wilson's debt was paid. So he should set this Silver girl down and walk away.

As though she sensed his intentions, she wrapped her arms around his neck. He could've easily broken her hold. Instead, he pulled her closer.

That's when Wilson knew that he was good and trapped.

Want to know who this mysterious Silver sister who just fell into her true love's arms is? You'll find out in "His Pledge to Protect," the third book in The Silver Star Ranch romances!

Grab your copy now!

Shanae Johnson was raised by Saturday Morning cartoons and After School Specials. She still doesn't understand why there isn't a life lesson that ties the issues of the day together just before bedtime. While she's still waiting for the meaning of it all, she writes stories to try and figure it all out. Her books are wholesome and sweet, but her are heroes are hot and heroines are full of sass!

And by the way, the E elongates the A. So it's pronounced Shan-aaaaaaaa. Perfect for a hero to call out across the moors, or up to a balcony, or to blare outside her window on a boombox. If you hear him calling her name, please send him her way!

You can sign up for Shanae's Reader Group and receive a FREE NOVELLA in this world at

http://bit.ly/ShanaeJohnsonReaders

Also By Shanae Johnson

The Silver Star Ranch Romances

His Pledge to Honor

His Pledge to Cherish

His Pledge to Protect

His Pledge to Obey

His Pledge to Have

His Pledge to Hold

The Rangers of Purple Heart

The Rancher takes his Convenient Bride

The Rancher takes his Best Friend's Sister

The Rancher takes his Runaway Bride

The Rancher takes his Star Crossed Love

The Rancher takes his Love at First Sight

The Rancher takes his Last Chance at Love

The Brides of Purple Heart

On His Bended Knee

Hand Over His Heart

Offering His Arm

His Permanent Scar

Having His Back

In Over His Head

Always On His Mind

Every Step He Takes

In His Good Hands

Light Up His Life

Strength to Stand

The Rebel Royals series

The King and the Kindergarten Teacher

The Prince and the Pie Maker

The Duke and the DJ

The Marquis and the Magician's Assistant

The Princess and the Principal

~

Made in the USA
Las Vegas, NV
26 March 2022

46368681R00106